CHANNEL

Editors:

Cassia Gaden Gilmartin and Elizabeth Murtough

Irish Language Editor/ Eagarthóir Gaeilge:

Aisling Ní Choibheanaigh Nic Eoin

Published with assistance from Publishing Intern S.R. Westvik.

Published in Dublin, Ireland by *Channel*.

Printed by City Print Limited.

Design and layout by Cassia Gaden Gilmartin.

Cover art by Bassam Issa Al-Sabah.

Cover design by Elizabeth Murtough.

ISBN 978-1-9162245-8-2

ISSN 2712-0015

Connect with us: www.channelmag.org | info@channelmag.org

facebook.com/ChannelLiteraryMagazine/ | twitter: @Channel_LitMag |

instagram: @channel_mag

Channel receives financial assistance from the Arts Council.

The position of Irish Language Editor/Eagarthóir Gaeilge is funded by Foras na Gaeilge.

Foras na Gaeilge

Fiction

Essay

Poetry

Cover Art: Still from *Dissolving Beyond The Worm Moon* by Bassam Issa Al-Sabah

Bassam Issa Al-Sabah works across digital animation, painting, sculpture and textiles creating visions of resistance, transformation and queer possibility. He completed a BA in Visual Art Practice from Dún Laoghaire Institute of Art, Design and Technology in 2016. Recent solo exhibitions include: *IT'S DANGEROUS TO GO ALONE! TAKE THIS*, The Douglas Hyde Gallery (2022); *I AM ERROR*, Gasworks, London (2021), and De La Warr Pavilion, Sussex (2022); *Dissolving Beyond The Worm Moon*, Solstice Arts Centre, Navan (2019); and *Illusions of Love Dyed by Sunset*, The LAB, Dublin (2018). Recent group exhibitions include *Queer Embodiment and Social Fabric* at the Irish Museum of Modern Art (2021–2022), The Dock, Carrick-on-Shannon (2021) and Golden Thread Gallery, Belfast (2020). Recent screenings include the Barbican, London (2022), Transmediale, Berlin (2021), EXiS, South Korea (2021) and Jeu de Paume, Paris (2021). His work is part of collections in IMMA, the Arts Council and Dún Laoghaire-Rathdown County Council. In 2021 he received the Golden Fleece Award, and he is currently a studio member at Temple Bar Gallery + Studios. Issa lives and works in Belfast and Dublin.

Note from the Editors

When we started *Channel* in 2019, we were drawn into the work by our mutual love of the natural world, of language, of the energy of relationship that underlies all things, and of the interplay between human and non-human creativity that shapes the environments we live within. Of these, we rely on language in particular as the mode of expression at the heart of our practice – as a medium for engaging with these other elements, a way to call out and call in their interconnectedness and, in so doing, foster a more conscious, participative way of being in the world.

We've been keen across our history to work with and publish authors in translation, and to explore the potential inherent in each piece's linguistic source. Each language, we believe, holds vital, original energies that, like the people, plants, animals and landscapes they describe, have shaped and been shaped by their relation to the manifold agencies of the world. Speaking, writing, reading, singing and listening in each language offers us not only different stories and perspectives, but access to richly variegated ancestral ways of seeing and participating in the world and in the collective. Through language, we create and represent not just the concrete world around us, but a biocultural continuum that is then encoded into the minutiae of how we live our lives together. This continuum means that whenever we communicate, in whatever language, we never represent something in a way that is entirely new – we learn and express the world through a lens that's been shaped by the collective, by the archetypes that reside therein, by deep geological and cultural time.

In this way, when we hold words in our mouths, in our ears or on the page, we are likewise being held by the vast container of human and non-human history. "Reality is / a continuing / crystal current," sings Susan Bruce (p. 85), and in relation to this current, we can experience a sense of profound gratitude, comfort and vitalising energy. But what happens when the histories encoded in that current are histories of harm, of the brutalising energies of oppression and domination? "Before us being us here they executed someone," says the English-speaking narrator of Martha Ryan's 'Summer's End.' "Settler sounds sedimentary but the record reveals a vulcanian juncture" (p. 26). Is it possible for the current to be interrupted by such junctures, to become heavy with break-points where the energy has been compressed instead of expanded by human interaction? And in what ways does this limit our capacity not just for communication, but for conscious and subconscious relationship with ourselves, with each other and with the natural world? "English has its poised lilts that scorn me," Athira Unni's speaker tells us (p. 98). A language weighted with collective histories of violence, shaped around lacunae of unresolved or unacknowledged hurt, may feel like no more than "Living experience rendered / into flattened shapes on a page that speak / to your nerves or call / up ghosts" (Martha Ryan, pp. 29–30). Faced with this flattening, one path toward a regenerative communication with the world is to bring multiple languages, each with its own dimensionality and heritage, into communion with one another.

And so it's a great joy for us, with this issue, to introduce a sustained bilingual element into our work, in collaboration with our new Irish Language Editor/Eagarthóir Gaeilge, Aisling Ní Choibheanaigh Nic Eoin. Where one language struggles within the limits of its construction, another may offer new, expansive possibilities – and we feel, with the introduction of Ireland's native language into *Channel*'s pages, a profound opening. An exchange of Irish and Breton words in William James Ó hÍomhair's 'Bealtaine na Briotáine' – "faou," "feá," "derv," "dair" (p. 64) – brings to light the depth of both languages' shared roots. And, in 'Faoistín Cloch,' Julie Breathnach-Banwait's speaker traces her own words back to their source in the whispers of the land: "Ach b'óna clocha a shil an sioscadh is b'iad a mheall comhrá asam" (p. 42). Each of the pieces in Irish within this issue embodies, in its own way, the deep expressive potential of a language formed over millennia in close relation with the landscape and non-human life of this country.

Beyond showcasing the power of our languages as they have been used to date, though, each piece in this issue speaks to us as its own distinct contribution to the ongoing life-flow from which Irish and English have emerged. Each piece, a unique permutation of words never before combined in the same way, turns up new resonances. Many of the works in these pages stretch the boundaries of the languages in which they are written, questioning the assumptions around which meaning has been formed. "One can wolf," Aodán McCardle remarks, in the sense of "to devour or swallow greedily," but "I saw them playing with a traffic cone in the snow … To wolf then can be to joy!" (pp. 106–107). At times, in search of fuller expression, languages are mixed freely: "rún in Irish passes between purpose and mystery and even love," McCardle continues; "these wolves are [rún]ning in the snow and all that they are are(ing) is a mystery" (p. 107).

Crucially, throughout these works there continues to be room for listening, for human words to be informed by other voices. "It's the coral chanting underwater / telling us how it sounds / to want to stay alive" (Jennifer LoveGrove, p. 116), and "we do / hear the mangroves, their silence / which is just another word / for time" (Jaye Nasir, p. 113). In the hands of these writers, language shows itself to be more than a human tool. Instead, it appears as a vital field, co-created with all elements of the human and non-human continuum, limitless in its capacity to connect, to guide, to generate. It is the current that *Channel* itself exists to hold, "the river's surface that carries everything / including the Achaeans, including the Trojans" (Rory O'Sullivan, p. 44), where "waves are extracted and rewoven to look out for one another" (Susan Bruce, p. 83) and where "bright morning stars were rising / like in the song we were singing" (Gemma Cooper-Novack, p. 61).

A note from our Irish Language Editor/Eagarthóir Gaeilge, Aisling Ní Choibheanaigh Nic Eoin

As I write this, it is mid-July and the summer seems to be fading. The clouds are pushing down against us, floods of rainwater are gathering in ditches along the road, that deep blue of evening is coming sooner each day. With this change in weather, our behaviours are changing too. Clothes are swiped off the washing line and left to dry inside, t-shirts are swapped for heavy rain-jackets and people run, under glowing street lamps, to get out of the weather. And again, on the cusp of a seasonal change, we are reminded that our lives are shaped almost entirely by our environment.

With these darkening evenings I am reminded of the generations that have come before us, of communal fires and the many millions of people who have sat around them, weaving together a rich tapestry of music, cultural celebration, and of course, language. The threads used for this tapestry are many, and they are so intricately connected that they have now blended into one piece of fabric. They are musical, lyrical, flavourful, and their greatest strength lies in their connection to one another.

For *Channel* to be embarking upon this new journey with the Irish language reflects this strength, and this connection. Shaped by the sharp rocks in the Atlantic, by the scent of bog plants, by the hands of countless families and communities, Irish is a language created by and within its own environment. It grows around the roots of yew, hazel and oak; in the seeds of spear thistle and foxgloves; in the green juice of nettles. It grows in the songs of school-children, and in the woven centre of crosses we make for Brigid. It continues growing, against all the odds.

Within these pages, we celebrate this growth. Here, the incredible and vivid life-force of our Irish language pieces will join a selection of beautiful English works to form the first bilingual issue that *Channel* has published, thus placing both languages in dialogue with one another. Here, stories of the plants we walk among, the seas we swim in, the names by which we call places, the traditions that we share with our friends in these islands, and all those fierce elemental features that have shaped this environment are becoming one new thread of this rich tapestry. As we look ahead to the warmth of fires, to music in dark pubs, to whisperings of our language echoing in rooms both here and abroad, to those black skies held off by laughter and song, our hands are raised to take this impossibly old tapestry from the generations before us.

And now we must learn to weave.

Beth McDonough

Crataegus

Fold up all news of uncertain use.
Hope slips into a printed tissue named *perhaps*,
to promote notes of variant thoughts.

We must unmask into cycling time,
face throttling winds and that lorry's filthy draught.
Turn to the salted air we need.

May gives us more than scent. Swallow that acrid,
throat-back taste from thickened green nearby.
Let branches stay outside. Intact.

Stella Reed

Edict

Let wind that stills our loneliness contain
 the restlessness of birds.
 Let trees holy to our longing and be firm.
Let green be a body.
Mercy found in scars.

If in this minute there is peace that does not last,
 let cottonwoods rattle brown leaves.

If night is another word for retreat, let stars break into our refuge.
If wind pushing water across the loch changes from clear to black,
 let the tonguing of sounds define.
Let the clamor quiet.
Let breath come back floating like clouds between mountain peaks.

If water is another word for life, let our souls be as fish.
If the word within the word within the word tethers us,
 let the calligraphy be ash, alder, birch.

If water is another word for life, let our joy be its reflection.

Stella Reed

Leaving Iona

Light fragments through the windows beneath a vaulted ceiling.
My right eye goes blind.

When I was a child I stared at the sun and followed
paths of red through a dark river.
In a small boat I rocked my way downstream
until I met the stone shore of sleep.

An ocean of time is a myth, a strand of hair cut at the knot.
I've carried your bones across a country clouded and green,
your open mouth filled with sea wind and gorse.

Once a woman held her hands to her eyes, shading
the sun as she searched the waves for her beloved.
Her effigy stands grey on the hill of Inverness. Her love
a myth cut through with storm.

Once I held a shard of glass and wished to go away.
The myth of my body cut through with time.
Now when I stand on the edge of a cliff I feel like flying.

I light a candle in the cathedral for the ones departed.
Smoke from the match curls upward like a ghost.
I believe it was my soul that rode the black river in a small boat,
smaller than the one that leaves Iona.

When the ferry meets the harbor, the church bells are ringing.
Something in me gives with the sound,
with the birds in the changing light.

Susan Lanigan

Rosa at Garryvoe, January '22

The beach gleams in sharp, winter light. The tide is going out, retreating towards Ballycotton Lighthouse. A nippy breeze plays on Rosa's skin as she walks barefoot over the luminous, blue swamp the sea has left behind. Her clothes are neatly rolled in a black canvas rucksack near the steps to the car park, where her battered Nissan Micra looks on, its windows blank. Goose pimples ripple on her thighs, her ageing knock-knees converging. Her swimming costume, a black one-piece with shorts, does nothing for the cold. Above, clouds race in a washed-out, egg-blue sky. The hotel on the other side of the road is quiet. Good. Better to avoid attention. She has not bared much since her separation last year. Now, after six months on medication, her body is different, feels the cold more, while her breasts have a new tenderness to them, both alarming and affirming.

Those pills and injectables, furtively ordered online, brought that tenderness to her heart as well. Everything is wondrous and painful. For the first time in her life, she feels fully human. But at a high cost. As she picks her way over the small stones and slippery seaweed, the voices start once more:

Ridiculous carry-on. You're a joke. A man in a dress.

How often do you masturbate? We need to know before we prescribe you anything. Why should we accommodate your delusional fetish?

"Fuck off," she says, clearly and firmly, her words not quite whipped away by the wind. A seagull wheels an arc on the same south-westerly gust, screeching *free, free*. Rosa keeps going, the saltwater lapping at her ankles, shins, knees, thighs, then –

She stubs her toe on a stone, loses balance, and falls in with an almighty splash. But while she is kicking and struggling and swearing and spitting out salt, she realises it's supporting her. The water.

She is swimming.

Exaltation surges within her. She rolls onto her back, floats. The sun comes out, brightness fractured in her water-speckled vision. What's causing this feeling? The oestrogen? The cold?

Or is it that she is life, woman, mammal, fish; all curve and wave, softened like a glass pebble that was once a beer bottle, but was then carried by the sea for a hundred years until being gently left on a beach to glint brown, blue, aquamarine? A mermaid, turned back to pure foam, no longer forced to walk on blades? Is it that the sea bears her weight, her changing body, her censured shape, without judgement? Or that the same sea, worn out with human ordure, poison, life-choking plastic, miles of it, can still find room for her, still, among the acidifying heat and relentless statistics, make her anew?

I am allowed to be here.

Kicking a lopsided breaststroke, Rosa swims on towards the horizon, perhaps beyond, to a world where human hands are kinder and more merciful, where the gods will joyfully forgive her transformation.

Sooner or later, she will come back ashore. But not yet.

Nils Nelson

Wild Fennel

It's not too dark
starlight gives us
what little we need

this path and these
forgotten train tracks
rusted bent overcome
with wild fennel

rub a sprig between

your palms
oil of licorice
heat from its fire

fills us now we can
each take a rail see
how far we can go

rolling the moments
up like sleeves
on a warm night

go ahead lick
the salt on your arm

come closer let me
enter the ocean
just above your wrist

Keev Ó Baoill

cois farraige, i bhfad uaim

Nuair a smaoiním ar an
bhfarraige, cuimhním ar mo mhamó,
                    ar mo fhíorghrá
's ar an tslí go mbreá leo beirt a bheith cois trá

Thosaigh muid amach, mo ghrá agus mé féin, mar chairde,
                    ag dul ag snámh cois farraige i mBrí Chualann,
        ag breathnú go cúthalach ar a chéile,
go rúnda

Muid ag siúil go sciobtha thar na clocha,

                    isteach san uisce linn agus í brathfhuar

Muid támáilte lena chéile ag an dtosach, iadsan ag féachaint orm go ciúin
    agus mé ag
gléasadh, fleasc caife eadrain
            Fuacht an fhómhair dá mo bhrostú

Cuimhním ar mo mhamó, agus í ag praeitseáil faoi bhuntáistí na farraige,
                    í ag insint dom nach bhfuil rud ar bith
                    níos deise don
                codladh, don sláinte, nó don ghruaig ná siúilín
                beag cois
                farraige,

fiú amháin do chosa a thumadh go
sciobtha
isteach san uisce; go gcaithfidh tú do
cheann a thumadh
san uisce freisin 's tú ag snámh
sin an rud is tábhachtaí
nach snámh ceart atá ann má tá culaith fhliuch bainteach
leis

Smaoiním anois uirthi, agus an fharraige i bhfad uaim, agus ise imithe
uaim freisin

Smaoiním uirthi agus mé ag siúil lámh le lámh le mo ghrá, i gcathair i
bhfad ón trá, ón
bhfarraige
ceistím cad a cheapadh sí fuaim anois 's faoi mo ghrá, muid beirt
ag brath an
fharraige uainn go mór

Smaoiním uirthi agus mé a siúil lámh le lámh le mo ghrá, i gcathair i
bhfad ón trá, agus muid
ag éisteacht le fear éigin ag béicíl rud éigin nimhneamh, úrghránna orainn

lover boys

is dócha go raibh sé an uair sin,
cad a cheapadh sí fuaim anois
'is faoi mo ghrá

Smaoiním ar an oíche chiúin sin gur shuí mé cois farraige sa Charraig
Dubh le mo ghrá,
muid cáirde amháin go fóill ag an stáitse seo,

agus muid písín ólta ag breathnú amach ar an bhfarraige,

KEEV Ó BAOILL

ag cómhrá eadrain féin, mise ag breathnú orthu go ceanúil, an tuiscint
   agam go raibh rud
éigin ag tarlúnt eadrain

Smaoiním ar mo mhamó ag suí cois trá i mBaile an Bhuinneánaigh, ag
   gáire 's ag caint go
mear le gach éinne thart timpeall, agus mise mar pháiste ag rith isteach
   san uisce, thar an
ngaineamh bog
      ní raibh áit ar bith níos deise i mo thuaraimse, 's mé i mo pháiste,
         ná an áit sin
Agus smaoiním arís ar mo fhíorghrá, agus an grá atá againn dá chéile,
   ag snámh go faiteach
i Muir na hÉireann
            ag siúil go seolta i gcathair i bhfad ón bhfarraige sin

Keev Ó Baoill

beside the sea, far from me

When I think of the
sea, I remember my grandmother,
                    and my true love
and the way they both loved to be by the ocean

We started out, my love and myself, as friends,
                    going swimming at the beach in Bray,

        looking shyly at one another,
secretly

Walking nimbly along those rocks,

                    into the water with us, good and cold

We were slow with each other at the start, them looking at me quietly
    while I was
dressing, a flask of coffee between us
            That autumn cold hurrying me on,

I remember my grandmother, her preaching about the benefits of sea
    water,
                        her telling me that there is nothing better
                            for the
                        sleep, the health or the hair than a little walk by
                        the ocean,

>   to immerse your feet quickly
>   in the water; to sink your head completely
>   below it also when you're swimming
>   *that's the most important thing*
> It isn't a real swim if there's a wetsuit involved

I think of her now, the sea far from me, and her gone from me too,

I think of her as I walk hand in hand with my love, in a city far from
    that beach, far from the
ocean,
        I ask what she would think of me now, and of my love, us both
missing the sea desperately

I think of her as I walk hand in hand with my love, in a city far from
    the ocean, and us
listening to some man shout something poisonous and nasty at us,

>   *lover boys*

I suppose it was that time,

>   *What would she think of me now,*
>   *and about my love,*

I remember that quiet night when I sat with my love at Carraig Dubh,
only friends at this stage,

>   and us pissed drunk looking out at the sea

talking to each other, me looking at them affectionately, understanding
that something was happening between us,

I think of my grandmother sitting on the beach in Ballybunion, laughing
and talking livelily about the sea with those around her, and me, as a
    child, running into that water, over the
soft sand,
        nowhere was better in my young mind, than that place

I think again of my true love, and the love we share, swimming timidly in
the Irish sea
            and walking lightly in a city far from that ocean

Seth Crook

Loving One Twin

A baltic tellin, not a trough shell.
An identification that pleases me,
like working out how to play a favourite riff.
I was vague about tellins, but now know.

Slowly, I distinguish between the species,
see each shell as an exploration of a form.
Even a small, hard-to-define difference
is sometimes enough for love.

G.G. Silverman

Ursus

A white circus bear sits in your living room and you can't fathom how it got there. Okay, maybe you do know. You leave the door unlocked every night because you feel safe in this small rural town, where you fled after your first post-grad job in the city didn't work out. But that still doesn't explain the larger sense of how, as in, what is a circus bear doing in your living room?

The bear remains polite, hands folded in his lap like, well, a trained bear. *I was abused*, he says, mouth not moving, but communicating with his thoughts. "And so one day," he continues, "after giving my handler the finger—something I learned by watching the kids in the audience—I made my escape. And here I am."

You wear your ex's boxer shorts and t-shirt as pajamas, and your bare feet are cold. You have nightmares when your feet are cold. Are you sleepwalking? You bite the hangnail on your left pinkie until it bleeds, and it hurts. You are definitely not sleepwalking. Are you hallucinating? You've been staying up late most nights working on your novel, drinking coffee spiked with whatever you can get your hands on that week in town.

Maybe. Maybe you're hallucinating.

"I've been watching you for a while," the bear says. "And I decided you were safe. You don't seem like the type to own a shotgun."

"No, I don't own a shotgun," you mumble.

"Well, great. Then I'm just going to make myself at home, right here."

You wonder how the creature picked up such colloquialisms as *well, great*.

"Okay," you say, voice feeble.

You stare at each other, attempting to ask questions.

Eventually, the bear tells you his name, the one given at the circus. It's not a name he enjoys. "It's Sparky," he says. "And it's insulting. Not even remotely capturing my essence."

"And please don't call me Bear," he says, "it's juvenile. Like a character in a kids' book. 'Bear picks up ball. Bear puts ball on his nose.' No, just no."

He pauses, releases a deep breath.

I am a rare white bear of the species Ursus americanus kermodei. The people of the land call me Moksgm'ol, or ghost bear. But you can call me Ursus.

"Ghost as in 'not really here,' or ghost as in white?"

"I assure you, I'm very real," Ursus says, still talking into your mind. He sighs. "Well, I'm really tired. Let's call it. Goodnight, and thanks for letting me crash."

He settles on your ratty old couch, the one you brought to college from your parents' basement and moved through several apartments. It still smells like your ex's sweat from countless nights making out, and then some. You make a mental note to have it cleaned, when you can scrape up some dimes. But now that Ursus has made it his bed, cleaning it would be for nought.

*

Over the next few days you're consumed by caring for Ursus, who doesn't want to be seen or found. He's ravenous, though, and skeletal—his pelt hangs on his bones. Scars trace his skin; his eyes hold circus tents of sorrow. You load your cart with salmon and berries at the Bargain Foodmart, noting that your savings are dwindling fast. The cart careens as you approach the white-haired cashier, who raises an eyebrow. You must love fish, she says.

As much as Ursus gorges, it's not enough. Soon, he's outside, even though it's risky for him to be seen, a big white bear like that. He claws the soil for bugs, and chomps grass and small animals—even roadkill. You breathe a sigh of relief when cars pass and Ursus is just out of view, mining your backyard for grubs.

Soon, he fleshes out into full bearness, and becomes magnificent. The sight of him no longer lashes your heart, if you can look just past the scars, squinting so they blend into fur.

Ursus is confused, though, by his humanity, the one that was forced on him, the neuroses and complexes often found in humans, now held by animals.

Most nights, he sits on your couch, which groans under his new weight. "I don't know who I am anymore," he says. "I've been through trauma, and need healing, I guess. That's it. Healing. Isn't that what you modern women call it?"

You nod. There are no therapists for bears. No one who could sit quietly and listen and offer solutions and advice to the bear out of touch with his wildness. It occurs to you that you've been thrust into this position—bear therapist—and you snicker. The snicker grows into full-on laughter, the hysterical kind, the kind you lapse into when high and watching cartoons.

"What?" Ursus says. "What's so funny? Is it something I said?"

"No, it's just me," you say, regaining composure.

"You know," Ursus says, "I used to get tired of being funny on command. Dancing on stools for the masses, only to be whipped later ..." His voice trails off, and he's lost in thought.

Meanwhile, you pop a bottle of cheap wine, 4-buck Chuck, and offer him a glass. Soon it's emptied, tossed, and you both drink from the bottle, straight-up not caring. You both titter, and Ursus stands. "Gimme your skirt," he slurs.

"What?"

"Gimme your skirt. Don't worry, I'm not being creepy, I just wanna show you somethin'."

Intrigued, you tear it off, and he paws it from you, attempting to wrap it around his body. "I used to have to wear skirts," he says. "Frilly ones. Tutus. And I hated it. But with you I feel safe ..."

He stands on the balls of his feet and rotates in a circle, tippy-toe ballerina-like.

You both laugh, you in your panties and Ursus in your skirt, and you pass the bottle back and forth, and he dances and dances, showing you everything he knows. How to be a ballerina, how to be a Cossack, how to be a whirling dervish. The sacred and the profane together in all that dancing. He shows you the can-can, shouting over his vigorous movement that this particular number is risqué, showing off legs and undergarments to the denizens of the underworld.

"Like me?" you say, kicking up your bare legs in time with his.

"Exactly!"

You dance and laugh and collapse on your couch in a great big heap of sweat and laughter and fur and you lean into him. You swig from another bottle. You're both warm and glowy and relaxed. You sigh deeply, playing with the fur on his chest. He grunts in contentment. You swear Ursus is blushing under that luxurious white coat, and your own body flushes red. He blinks; you're both quiet. You break the ice again by spooning into his side, feeling his warmth on your back.

After a time, Ursus speaks softly, as if lulling you to sleep. *It was once believed that bears gave birth to the universe. That we held all of creation within us, and every winter the universe slumbered inside the bear-mother's womb and was reborn. We were once sacred, revered. We were sung by the shaman, we bore the cradle of infinity. It was believed that we were the father of all men and that to kill a bear was to kill your own father, to kill your own next of kin.*

*

You and Ursus have the same dream—his mother's belly contained infinite galaxies, with all their stars, whirling nebulae, moons, and planets lush with oceans, trees, and animals. Every bird in the skies of multitudinous worlds flew from her cave of soft wet flesh. Every vine curled curious and hungry from the dark space in her center. Every flower burst forth, spreading seed. After every cycle around the sun, all of creation was reborn in this way, tumbling from the belly of his mother. You and Ursus wake and weep. His mother is no more.

*

The next morning, you're both awkward. Neither of you speak about what happened. Instead Ursus paces your shabby rug 'til it's threadbare.

"I should teach myself to fish," he announces. "You know what they say, that old adage, teach a man to fish, eat for a lifetime, etcetera, etcetera." He clears his throat.

"Yes," you blurt. "But do you feel safe out there? You said they were looking for you." They being the circus.

You realize too late that you've added to his neurosis, but the words have already launched from your mouth like bombs. Second guessing his instinct—the typical move of a codependent girlfriend.

"I don't know," he says. "I just … don't know." He shrinks against the couch, deflated.

Time for damage control. "You should do it!" you say. "Let's go!"

You find yourselves outside in the crisp cold of early morning. A brook with fish lurks somewhere off the edge of your property, you're sure of it. Ursus glances over his shoulder as he ambles toward the woods. Soon he lopes into a run on all fours, instincts kicking in. You struggle to keep up, but eventually catch him brook-side. He sniffs the air. The water bubbles and flows, and he watches, keen.

Hours go by with the river.

Not a single fish appears.

My mother once told a story, he says, the same story passed on by her own mother, and her grandmother's mother—of a time when the rivers teemed with flashing silver; the silent gods of the waters offered up the tender flesh of their bodies for us, so that we may eat of it and we may all be reborn. And the silent gods of silver came back year after year, as did we, waiting for them to swim up the river, to feed the mothers of all creation.

Ursus weeps—the silent gods are no more.

*

After the morning at the river, Ursus drowns his sorrow in drink. He refuses food. And there have been rumblings in town—a rare white bear has been spotted in the woods behind your home. An escaped circus bear. And there's a reward. Rednecks with rifles knock on your door. You peer through a knife-thin gap in the curtains. You know what they've been saying. You're the woman who loads her cart with an ungodly amount of fish at the market. What the hell are you doing with so much fish? And berries. God, so many berries.

You are paralyzed by empathy. Ursus falls into a long slumber, though it's not winter. And it's not restful sleep, but the kind where he curls up fetal, whimpering and twitching. You tear yourself away from watching him, forcing yourself to be useful. As you wash dishes, his nightmares bleed into your waking mind. Shadows of ringmasters with whips stretch past your consciousness. Stars blink out one by one; entire galaxies go dark. Every plant and tree shrivels backward to dust. Rivers and oceans desiccate; the last few fish gasp for air. There is no more wind, just an eerie cosmic silence. Death as far as the eye can see.

*

Wake up, Ursus.
Wake up, wake up, wake up.

*

When you're sure there's no one spying on your home, you rouse Ursus and smuggle him into your campervan, where tinted windows hide you from prying eyes. You drive for four, five hours, further and further into the national park at the northwestern tip of the U.S. You think of your ex, a hippy-dippy commitment-phobe, how when drunk he'd say that someday, as an old man, he'd end his life in the noblest way possible— not hooked up to a mass of tubes and machines, but by going into the woods, limping and shuffling, in the hopes of being wrestled by a bear, a worthy opponent, a god. At the time you thought it was stupid. But now you're not so sure.

Ursus begins shielding his thoughts, watching the landscape as the van penetrates wilderness. You think about things you've left behind because of their confinement: countless jobs, the city, four novel drafts in a drawer. Maybe your ex wasn't the commitment-phobe after all. Maybe you're the cage. You release your past with a deep breath, tires crunching gravel as you pull into a deserted parking lot by a trailhead. Van parked, you and Ursus sit, quiet. The evergreens are dense, dripping with moss. Ferns grow waist-high.

Finally, Ursus speaks. "It's time."

You're not sure if you should hug; it's too awkward to try in the van. You exit, and it occurs to you that unlike friends you've dropped off for hiking expeditions in the past, Ursus has nothing but the coat he was born in. No pack, no GPS, no maps, no trail mix, nothing. Only eyes and teeth, nose, claws, and wits. You want to say, "Be careful out there!" but you don't. You want to shout, "Stay safe!" but you shouldn't. He has everything he needs.

You stand at the trailhead, and Ursus' haunted look returns.

"This is my destiny," he asserts, growling away his feelings. "This is my medicine." He takes a sniff, then another, and relaxes visibly. He points to a tree. "Western red cedar." Another sniff, another point. "Giant sequoia."

Gravel crunches behind you. You turn and blink. You swear you hadn't seen anyone for miles. Yet an old man is walking up the lonely road with a cane, his coat, and nothing else. "Sorry, miss," the man calls out. "I'll wait my turn with the bear."

"No, no," you say, "I'm not in line."

"You're not waiting to …?"

"Nope. Just saying goodbye to a friend. He's all yours."

"Ah," the man says. "Thank you."

Taking your leave of Ursus, you pass the elder gentleman and catch his gaze. He reaches out to stop you, taking your arm for a moment in the clumsy way of old men. His expression, too, is haunted, not by circus tents of sorrow, but by vast zip codes of skyscrapers. "Be good," he tells you. "Live your best life."

You nod, fighting an unnamed emotion in your chest, then the old man shuffles behind you where Ursus waits for his first customer, his first worthy opponent. You slide back in your van, arm still warm from the man's touch. A thick patch of stray fur blesses the passenger seat, and a burst of loneliness grips you. You don't know if you'll ever be the same, but maybe you don't want to.

Through your window, you watch Ursus and the old man face each other, assessing the damage each has suffered, two ghosts seeking a cosmic twin.

Then, a bow and an introduction. *I am a rare white bear of the species Ursus americanus kermodei. The people of the land call me Moksgm'ol, or ghost bear. But you can call me Ursus.*

The man nods. Ursus points out another tree before going down on all fours and lumbering away in slow motion, the man shambling by his side. They disappear from the edge of your vision, swallowed up by ferns.

You close your eyes. Your van still smells like him, pungent and wild. The edges of time and space warp inside you, spilling backward and forward, no end, and no beginning. You imagine Ursus and his new friend, discussing philosophy and infinity and reincarnation before they come to the logical end of the trail, the place Ursus feels is the Right One. And they will lie there, soft with pine needles and hidden from the wind, and the old man will bury his face in Ursus' soft fur, and they will roll and tussle, the man hanging on not for dear life but for the sweet release of death, and Ursus will take the old man inside him, where he will not feel any more pain, but will tumble into a primordial darkness teeming with stardust, amidst galaxies and nebulae, waiting to be reborn.

Monica Wang

Tim was Our Cousin Who Liked Music and Sketching and Martial Arts Novels

whom we begged to take us to the woods, so we could go out
after dark. He never looked afraid, unlike us, we who stayed
away from the door past dark

We walked down to the basement, deep down to his room, distant
from the woods and our rooms (where we were watched
by our parents from their rooms)

All right, he said, though on other nights he'd said *no*, knowing
we weren't allowed, knowing we didn't think of him
or whether he was allowed

In the woods he led us down grey-lit and softly-mulched
unseen paths, held aside bramble and was duly scratched
turning steps to trodden path

In the light of the living room our parents yelled without
hitting him as they would us—they said hitting was love,
(only) they loved (only) us

As we hid in the corridor, shadows who watch, his face
looked nothing like theirs, our parents who didn't like the woods
or our uncle's kids or theirs

All my fault, he said, as if he liked demanding, cowering
cousins who couldn't see at all after dark, one of the last nights
he lived with us, in the dark.

Monica Wang

In November, a walking tour

Orange in a garnet month
the maples not flat red or orange
but tangerine and ruby edged in precious
metals. A young woman eats in a bent tree
with no leaves in front of a great hall
blunt under a sky less overcast than back
home. Leaves lie curled like daylilies underfoot
ready for stirfry as we cross a meadow on the side
of the hill, meek lambs mewling, "I thought
there was lunch." A path too narrow
for us; a bloom too bright; pinecones too large for the branches
they sit on—but none falls off as too-large trucks pass
us by the pond by the ditch by the busiest road
on campus. "It's fetid," someone says, then passes
around sandwiches. There is such thing as free lunch
after all, more than enough to go around.

Padma Thornlyre

Two Poems from *Her Glyphs (Rosaline, Book 1)*

A Cluster of Sweating Grapes
(Variations of Identity)

> *Recline*
> *and let me feed you, Rosaline,*
> *I am the cluster plucked from the vine*

Or let these stars be grapes that I might
crush them with you, that our flesh be

stained with the juice of those berries;

and let us grow wings. Or let me cool
your throat berry by berry, or warm

your belly with wine. Let me struggle
in the wind and colding night, let me
suckle the sun for you, suck minerals

from a soil so volcanic it has people
inside it, painters of swallows, painters

of dolphins, of lilies and blue monkeys.

Here is papyrus and the goddess bare-
breasted, a song we recall in silence.

GLYPH: grape cluster on gray stone

Woman As Labyrinth and What Is Held Within

I saw you, Rosaline,
atop a darkling wall, as
thistledown struck by the sun

To navigate her wounds, hoist anchor, light
a torch, walk backward (what beast resides

within her succumbs to honey), and bring

a lamb-gut. Pinion butterflies (no, not that),
and learn to play cat's cradle for the flesh-

memory of string between your fingers:
razor-hewn the horns you face. Gently, then.
Every fork secures a destiny. At the navel

of all waters set your weapons down, shed
your skins, recline in the darkness of her.

Here she will not harm you. If your tongue be

kind she will not harm you. For Naxos then,
and the vine-clad arms of her God, set sail.

GLYPH: labyrinth on bluish-gray stone

Martha Ryan

Summer's End

I.

At first there's much to say. In beginning there are necessities like setting. It's summer. My lover and I are going on a long trip. One long summer love—time to hose out the savings, hike in wilderness. We want us a wildness free of motor vehicles.

While machineless we speak of location—where spoken, what tongue? English American English we speak we exchange as we explore we execute what we mean.

Before: before us being us here they executed someone. Someones. Settler sounds sedimentary but the record reveals a vulcanian juncture: blasted life and limb into air where it still hangs, ashen. And reconcile? Reform? Remembering?

I'll admit that we're getting lost.

Relevant: where we're going, lost. We embark from the forest edge along the trail through conifers, shady and mute atop dropped fir needles. We traverse sierra labia—the rock folding batter into itself—until somewhere along the sealed ridge lip we lose ourselves.

Once lost we're seeking any trail road town where we'll find cell service. We're going—

Irrelevant: how we got here—no record of how we lost. The fact is loss. Where lost what we lost we're going to keep going to Corpolis, WY.

That place I spot on my map as the closest clot of roads, you know, rides.

Shortcut to Corpolis is easy! says the lone hiker we encounter who sinews past us, her hiking poles tenderizing the ground.

Not far? Only a couple hours? We'd planned for a full day of dust in boots huffing in altitude dazed my breathless dirty dream. We watch the clouds puppeteer a tale atop the quartzite face rouged with feldspar smudge.

We thank our friend all cheery spirits and reassurance we're taking a shortcut we'll get there in no time. We wander slow. We're always allochthonous: displaced, absolutely, from our sites of formation: fissured by deep time.

Time passes no Corpolis no road. We still we wander we pleasure we delay slow easy steps along some river is that crystal is that quartz? What's caught in lithic obscurity what's stuck here
in the batholith.

II.

Once I found my language
useless. Have you? I spoke
wrongly that is, in ways
no one got.

I grew slack but repetitive. However words arrived in my head I'd say aloud like that. And then say it again adjust some however. And then, I grew slack to myself repeating. To repeating myself. To saying what I meant, different. Making sure you get it? I said same things a lot.

III.

Before summer hit I tried to write about the pandemic that had halted life. But I couldn't. I was waiting to write about it because it wasn't over yet. And during the first lockdown, everyone else was writing about it anyway: *Humans are the real virus. The earth is healing in our absence—*

remember those revelations that we saw ourselves as separate from land?

IV.

the neurologist told me fear not fear NOT. dr. neuro showed me charts
told me pain means only
pain. told me brain not dumb. NOT dumb but nerves they lick old
wounds? nerves haha too sentimental. NOT nerv*ous* no no.
shhhhh to my nerve. chemical SHUSH to my nerves. NOT nervous no.
my nerve sounds in no language
other than my own burn prior. i vomit on doc's creased loafers i syncope
floor flat i'm bedridden sleepless caught in my body like that i thought
often of endings
dr. neuro shows a scan says you want to surger? will it end? i spit i spy
no finale hidden deep in my cranial jelly making
deals helped sometimes. imagine the longest time endurable. no—
be reasonable. vomiting down to the gallbladder green takes about
twelve hours i that is you i mean me rather i i strike a deal for ten then
tell myself: only five hours until i'm halfway through.

III.

During the lockdown, I wasn't waiting for a return to *normal* per se—just
a movement to a different place. Different enough to foster perspective,
hindsight. I've gone through plenty of change during the pandemic, but
nothing large or complete enough to tell a full story. Not transformational
enough to think, okay, now. I'm different now. The change so slow I forget
who I was before, who I was when I started telling myself the story of myself.

I.

Here in batholith hours pass igneously. To make batholith, you know, you
need a lot of dikes fingering along sedimented bodies. Check and check.
I piss the last of my water out, wonder who and what I'm watering. One

dyke pees into Earth while another dike gurgles magma back. While I squat among grass dry as tibia I stare out at the canyon's chip-tooth grin. The fractured columns below cling to nothing in mid-plunge.

Here her and I drink less.

Here are hours passing.

No Corpolis no road time passes I lithify we shuffle. Time shuffles my mouth dry my words brittle my bottle empty the creek suddenly far below—how did we drift so far so waterless? I was benthic once: once I entered a love so abyssal it flooded me full of silt and brine.

Now my boots heavy like they must've stayed sodden in secret. 11,000 years of human presence and here we stride in sun's midday that strikes the tributary's bleed into bigger river but so far below my alpine shamble no words remain. We trudge along silence.

My footsteps mark a line, a curvy, digressing line from one unknown to another. I drag myself along an unplanned line of flat-footed ancestry.

What came before, before then, before then? An inexact science, trying to prove everything invented. But my family name's German, that is, some men before my time kept this one small strand alive. At least one man who left his family home; his son or son of son who eventually landed in this country, where he would become unambiguously white, a blood-eyed weaponry.

A fearful confrontation with past.

II.

Is language its own
ending? Living experience rendered
into flattened shapes on a page that speak

to your nerves or call
up ghosts: those who seduce
and mingle with your own memory your own
life, your time.

I.

Finally: a fire road, the valley grass interrupted by smooth humanized
pebble—a motor growls behind. Finally!
My mouth droughted—we must be close after all.
I say aloud. Thank god we weren't so far.

White truck pulls over. Do we need help? Not usual to find hikers in
these parts. Or—not usual to find parts on these hikes.

We confer. Already found a road. Road must lead to imminent opolis.
Probably fine.
Rather not risk the men in a white truck risks.
We decline, continue on. Thirst returns—the river taunts distantly. We
walk road curves closer to water I say
      Thank god the river's getting closer.

IV.

how much: how much time left life breath how long until what's here ends

i learned my first pain tricks in competition, in running. after four loops
around the football field only four pains more. or cross country: at the
halfway point i just needed to come back home.
i got a rock that's good for being halfway i press its steeple into my brow it
goes on it keeps going on i press until the outer starts to match the dull inner

races end and satisfy—line to cross, medals and pedestals. but
neuralgia   ? not yet olympic. haha. in pain no telling which bout

of vomiting is last. i waked from unconsciousness the fact of sleep itself hallmarking pain's peter outward. a sputter back to life if i sat up   if i sat up   once i sat up too quickly

i wish it meant. it denies definition—you sit wait for me to name it something: science too small a way to know

though i hated the pain i hated more the anticlimax:

I.

From one dike to another I'll share a secret: I can't keep much contained.

On our dyke hike I've begun spilling again a story I often tell. I exsolve it when there's acute craving for a closure.

It's a story I tell myself; I story me. It's not mine until it is. Once I lifted it from someone's book, I held it in my gut fractionated it fossilized. It's a haunting story. I can't stop retelling it. Do I begin again? The allure of the horror is that it's someone else's. It's not mine until it is.

My lover wishes I would stop it. In our years together I have started it again and again, rarely finished. I start it when we find ourselves in long lines or when we camp and feel a little frightened of the sounds around.

She hates the story because halfway through, or three-quarters, or sometimes right during the dénouement, I remember something I forgot. A crucial detail. Something key for the ending to hit. I'll revise mid-way. Remember when I said this? It was actually that.

My lover wants a straighter story, one that ends efficiently.

She hates the way I tell the story because I take a long time telling it. So long that I lose myself along the way. I love the details, what the dead cat's innards look like. I draw unnecessary comparisons. Remember our neighbor lady who had teeth like dried corn? Mrs. Poroth had a grin like that.

She hates it because I won't stop trying to tell the story until I get the ending right. The ending is the only part I remember very clearly.

I.

In Bosnia, Cambodia, Germany, Peru, Rwanda. Sites where the violence was preserved. Museums, galleries of memory. Does it help? Who gets helped? What does it do? Is there an entry fee?

Museums love stories with endings, stories voice-overable by a calm British accent. Would an American museum dare start a story that it can't finish? What's the entry fee of denial? What's the entry fee of truth?

Water down below snakes a pale green vein.

II.

Is a word dead?

III.

A pandemic change: my intimacy with death. Deaths of specific people— family members, friends, friends' family members, and so on, who have passed away during the recent years or who I worry about. Deaths of animals and trees as I watch the wildfire smoke from my sealed window. Deaths of species as I scroll through the news again, looking for something cheerier than Instagram obituaries.

I.

Now I watch my love's stopped-up pores gemmed in her plutonic cheek, the way she erupts, do you think we're going to die? So I don't ask permission to begin the story I can't end.

In beginning there are necessities like setting. Once there was a woman who traveled to the Poroth Family Farm. I always begin the same way. The woman had a lot of reading to do. These are the books she brought. She's staying in a cabin in the woods, renting from people she's never met. Mrs. Poroth never speaks but grins widely. Her open mouth reveals twisted dental geography: dried corn planted in rough rows. You remember our neighbor? Like that.

The white truck behind us again.
How did they?
Behind us again?
Followed?
This time scornful—rude hand gestures, teasing.

Did we fuck up?
Yes, we decide.
Mistakes were made.
Something sunk.

A choice: go completely colloidal among friendly sediments or risk anthropogenic wound?

Thirst triumphs.

Take off running wave the guys down: please help us. This moment preceded us particular foreigners of this land: our foreignness precedes us, our asking for help in here echoes something older. We're in the truck I speak quickly my voice restored: close call. Could have been bad. Thank god we're finally going to Corpolis.

II.

When became I illegible I lost
in the moment of speech.
If I speak incohered is it anything
other than white noise?

I.

We: her, me, him, him, driver drive in silence until the road ends. No
warning just ending
the road stops where the cliff starts, river flashes far below in reptilian blues.

No bridge, neither for cars nor feet. Only a small wood box suspended
over the river. A thick wire is all that holds the box aloft. We stare, we sweat.

We ask the stupid question: where's the bridge? Where's the bridge?
Where's your brain? It's the fruit box across the river or a sleep on the
side of the road.

We want more time to decide.

Get in it.
There's a car on the other side.
It won't wait long.
Hurry up.

Strung between the Laramide and Sevier orogens, we lost among glacial
carving. Heat—I'm sweating—oceanic friction birthed this granite erodes
to river salty river. Tip the vertical horizonal, as the box sways, and make
fresh jags. Mélange me, I beg, you zone of mudstone:

Two of us boxed clutch backpacks above our heads. Terror consumes
me in the middle.

If the box stops mid-wire?
If the rope breaks?

Hung in fear no past no future.

Finally! The river's other bank. My legs quaking I seize to the car, a
woman gets in the driver's seat, some men inside waiting. When the
engine starts relief floods. I say to my lover: thank goodness that could
have been catastrophic. I'm glad we made it. Hey, my lover says, can
you stop putting cherries on top?

III.

My thoughts about death are mostly abstract, until my grandmother dies,
and then there's just pain and confusion. There aren't words. There
aren't long stories. There are hard potato chips that cut my cheek and
uglier flowers than I expected.

When I return home after the funeral, it's a marvel to watch how fast I
slide back into abstractions. Death is the eventual mystery, the primordial
origin, the places we are always suspended in between.

When I zoom out far enough, or take enough drugs, I convince myself
that death is a neat and tidy ending.

II.

Is a word dead?
Is a body never dying?

I.

An hour in the car, an hour and a half.

I keep up the fearful tale to my lover: our protagonist feels something's off. Something on the farm is a little bit off. But there's no evidence, nothing set in stone. So she suppresses her perturbations. Yes, the pressure builds.

One passenger departs, to my eye, in the middle of nowhere. We drive, nowhere: the barely-there road clings on the mountain gut.

Sandstones slates lavas tuffs below above around.

Past a station of backcountry jeeps. Corpolis? We ask. No, no, not yet. This is not Corpolis. This is large scale breccia, unmappable body of rock.

III.

Within the first few weeks of the illness creeping across the country, I heard there were shortages of pain medications. An early rumor: don't take ibuprofen if you have the sickness. So I scoured the sold-out pharmacies for bottles of Tylenol. How much would I need to see through disease? I thought maybe two bottles i.e. two weeks.

I.

Keep driving. The other passengers descend. Silence, then the upbeat country song fuzzing into radio range, and then out of it.

Finally, when it's just us and the driver, she says she's heading up to a remote mountain town, and do we want to come? Otherwise, she can just drop us by a small group of RVs on the horizon.

What? We misperceived, misunderstood. Not going to Corpolis?
Oh no, we passed Corpolis long ago.

Miscalculation. Oops. We are once again lost—she pulls over and asks a man operating a bulldozer if he can let us use his phone. Yes. Oh yes, he can.

MARTHA RYAN

We get out. When we ask the bulldozer-er tosses us a crumpled plastic water bottle. I'm awash with adrenaline and relief.

Thank god we made it out before she drove us deeper in the loss. We got this water. We had some close calls but now we are finally safe—

Baby, says my lover, it's not over yet.

IV.

fuck. in pain in land of pain in land of fuck oh fuck make it stop please

nurse enters—please god please stop it

tries to find a vein in the vein the vein pumping pain through my spine

well well. says nurse god of pain. well you DO have these tiny veins hey?

venipuncture horribly. blood trickles down my elbow crease, i watch it fall i wonder is that
me
now
ending? i need the needle to free me but the needle hits dry land again again again oh fuck.

when's the last time asks god since you've had water? WELL no wonder if you've been

vomiting every ten minutes. let me get elisha she's good with this stuff.

II.

Is a word dead?

Is a body never dying?

Is a story ever over?

I.

It's not: the bulldozer operator says words unfathomable. Broke cell phone, also, now I think of it, usually no service.

He points back roadside says try that. Try to get a lift from any late hunters. I'm deepening desperation. I sip deepening water. We wait. My sediments stirred up again. My stirrings sedimenting.

While waiting I keep speaking: our protagonist waits and waits. She waits for a sign or a symbol. She gets a weird feeling. She finds a cat grotesquely dead. Its innards look like charcuterie put in a blender. She decides this is neither sign nor symbol. She goes out alone in the dark night and waves her hands in a way she wishes would change something.

I know this part, says my lover.

III.

When I finally get the feared disease I battle virus by observation. I try to watch what happens closely. I try to let the thing I'm watching teach me how to see it. This becomes my practice of seeking ending: watching myself disappear and appear and change again.

IV.

elisha forgoes elbow crooks tries the river in my hand.
bless elisha deity of hope. elisha I owe you
my   .
sweet elisha evades my neural chaos makes a new mouth in my hand. in

flow fluids compounds that bind all biological my nerve endings suspended by elisha. elisha our lady of grace brings a warm blanket as i shiver from my bagged water drip chill saint elisha injects the hydromorphone into my new plastic throat.

II.

Does this mean anything to you?

I.

Rides pass that we decline. Truck with bed full of construction workers, nope, car of four men who grin and slow until we wave them on, no, no.

The hours lose hope as the sun dips behind the mountain ridge. A coming to terms with our impending rocky beds, stone pillows. Bedside cherts snoring out their silica.

II.

I still get episodes of excruciating
nerve pain. It's threatening
my spine as I write. There's no cure. To admit
that it happened I needed
to believe in its ending.

When the pain comes
there's no fear, just horror.
When the pain dies
the fear fills its absence.

How are we going to get through this?

Do you want me to end it?

IV.

once the hydromorphone hits i feel great. i mean fucking fantastic.
i don't recommend it lest you begin to fear endings
in addition to depending upon them.

I.

Finally: a red economy car zips around the road's curves. We wave it down when we see a woman driving. Stop please! Please stop! She rolls down the window.

Our predicament comes out breathless, anaerobic, though we've been at altitude long enough, too long, long time, little oxygen.

The woman nods and unlocks the doors. Her fingernails match the car's cherry paint. We pile in. I am relieved. I am, if I may, a subducting carbonate: edges blur I sink. My face free from the mountain precipitates— saltwater erodes through my dusted crag.

Goodbye to bulldozer and the man with his deadened phone.

This time this eon I keep my mouth shut. We drive to Corpolis in silence. When we ask if she'll take some money as thanks, she says as you wish. We do.

I wait until we check in to a motel before I finish my horror story. It's a quick ending: the protagonist winds up sweating inside a cheap motel. There's something coming for her, something like a zombie, something that can infect people and convert them into evil beings with red eyes. She has locked the door. She has called a news reporter to sound the alarm. She's trying not to panic that it's all too late, that she's accidentally unleashed the force that will end the world, but when she pulls back her curtains there's a man sitting across the road, unmoving, waiting. When they lock eyes our protagonist sees her stalker has "eyes of blood."

MARTHA RYAN

Remember when I said that's the end? It's actually not. The last paragraph lays out, for anyone who might have missed it, exactly what the speaker fears has happened: that she "called down evil from the sky," everyone's deaths imminent, and that "the harvest is past, the summer is ended, and we are not saved."

When I finally finish the story I shudder like I did before. If you're telling a story, after all, don't you want to make sure your audience is getting your meaning, especially if the world's ending?

My lover takes photos during the hike, even during dehydration and altitude sickness. The pictures, in the aftermath, are mostly blurry and tilted—the frame too shaken by the hand.

This is the ending of my story. Here, we end. In this piece, I have done you a good deed of ending something uncomfortable. It's over now.
 I mean to say, I've lied to you.
 The harvest is past, the summer is ended, and we are not saved.

The horror story referred to is T.E.D. Klein's novella The Events at Poroth Farm.

Julie Breathnach-Banwait

Faoistín Cloch

Bhí rud éigin faoin ngaoth sin a ghlaoigh. An t-olagón caointeach cráite úd, do choinneáil ar an airdeall i ndubh na hoíche, ar fhaitíos go mbeadh duine ró-shocraithe. Is an talamh leis. Seasc feannta, is gan maithiúnas. Go mba leis an anam amháin í. Gan bia ná deoch á thairiscint aici ach gur bheathaigh sí anam cráite. Ba í an ghaoth úd a d'fhág balbh gan smid mé.

Ach b'óna clocha a shil an sioscadh is b'iad a mheall comhrá asam. Gur shéid siad thríom lán an bhéil d'fhocail is d'úrnaí le teannadh. Lena raimhreacht, lena scraitheanna bána cnis, lena ngoba géara, caonach clúdaithe mar phluid ghlas. Is nuair a scoilt siad, istigh iontu a bhí croí an loinnreach. Solas nach thuigeas ariamh a thomhais, glaineacht is boigeacht craicinn páiste nua-bheirthe ina gceartlár. Bhí sióga ársa ár sinsir iontu ina suí mar bhreithiúnaí sagairt, fealsúnach is frithchaiteach, scáileach smaointeach, is lena gcuid méara lúbtha gobacha a ghlaoigh siad chucu mé chun faoistine. Thóg na clocha siúd mo lámha is leagadar ar chuisle mo chroíse iad. Is ghlac siad le maistíneacht is le mianta. Le bás is beatha. Is gach smál ar mo cholainn. Is d'fhéach siad ar gach peaca a d'fhág a lorg. Is dúradar liom nach raibh ionam ach duine. Scaip siad mo laigeachtaí trasna na gcnoc is na gcnocán, go dtí nár aithin mé iad romham. Codlaím lena ndubh, déanaim brionglóid ar a nglas, éirím lena mbán. Impíonn a gcuid scailpeanna ar bhláthanna fás.

Is ghlaoigh comhrá na gcloch úd orm i gciúnas na hoíche. I nguthanna a cruthaíodh dhomsa amháin is i ndathanna nach ndamhsaíonn d'éinne ach mé. Le gach tuirling gréine, lagann a nglaoch go gol geoin, go sioscadh síodúla, go dtí go n-éistear liom is go dtiteann mo chorp i gciúnas buíoch.

Julie Breathnach-Banwait

Stone Confession

There was something about that wind that called. That sharp wail, agonising, kept alert at night for fear that one might be too settled. And the ground with it. Searing barrenness, and unforgiving. Belonging only to the soul. Not offering food or drink, but nourishing that anguished soul. She was that very wind that left me mute.

But from these rocks flowed whispers, and it was they that pulled speech from me. They that blew through me with a mouthful of words and vespers. With their succulence, with their scabs of white skin, with their sharp points, covered in moss like a green blanket. And when they split, inside them lay the heart of light. A light that will never be measurable, the cleanness and softness of a newborn child in its centre. The ancient fairies of our people were sitting like judicial priests, philosophical and reflective, in meditative shadows, and with sharp, bent fingers, they called me to confession. Those rocks took my hands and laid them on the pulse of my heart. They accepted bullying and desire. Life and death. And every blemish on my body. And they looked at every sin that's left. And they told me that I was only a person. They spread my weaknesses out across mountains and hills, until I no longer recognised them before me. I sleep with their black, dream on their green and rise with their white. Their crevices lure flowers to grow.

And the chorus of those rocks called me in the quiet of night. In voices generated for me only and in colours that dance for nobody but myself. With every sunset, their call weakens to a whimpering cry, to a smooth whisper, until they listen to me and my body falls into a grateful silence.

Rory O'Sullivan

Trojan Peace

Dawn in rain, mist on the sea, waves echoing.
The Myrmidons are leaving Troy: it means
victory for the Trojans, death for the Achaeans.

No one sleeps. They are watching Achilles
face-forward on the stern, hair shining back.
Next to him Patroclus strums a lyre, slaves
listen at their feet. The helmsman cries
at the boatsmen, ropes slack, sails high:
they are heading home.

They are heading to be forgotten.
They are like glow-worms on a tree
in Autumn that stop glowing as night
darkens. They are like mayflies drowned
on the river's surface that carries everything
including the Achaeans, including the Trojans.

They are like bees in a storm: bees
whose nest floods and they fly off,
scattered, then the storm finishes.

Rory O'Sullivan

Lament of the Wise

I was born without joy,
without love, without
kindness.

A wound, I was rancid
and drove people away.
Helpless

on my knees, I clawed
the earth. Beneath me
a chasm

formed, I lay down
for many years
listening:

it was night. Beside me
foxes shrieked, winds
roared

in the dark, my life
opened. Everything
I learned

I learned too late, I am old
too soon. Like a tree
my mind

stands rooted still
my thoughts like pollen
scatter.

Ion Corcos

On the Day the World Ends

after Jorge Teillier's The End of the World

The day the world ends the river will still be flowing
over worn stones, the white-throated dipper will scour
quiet water, the reeds will still be yellow.
A bicycle will be left against a wall.
The moon will appear in the daylight sky, and an eagle
will soar above the forest. A dog will bark.
In a restaurant, a waitress will lay a tablecloth,
plate, knife, fork and spoon, a paper napkin.
The mountains will stand above the town, and the museum
of the revolutionary poet, Nikola Vaptsarov, will open
as usual, and the square will still hold his name.
Stray kittens will perch on a shed roof and meow.
A man will order a bowl of lentil soup, with fresh bread,
and a plate of fried cabbage. There will still be agreements signed
to sell arms, and bombs will be dropped on civilians,
indiscriminately. Tongues will still rattle. Yemen
will remain an unknown name. Pumpkins will grow.
Spring onions will still sprout. And a thoughtless man
will trip over himself. The idea of a sunflower field will arise,
and the history of metaphysics will erupt into flames.
A horse will calmly roam among trees, hidden streams,
graze alongside two other horses, watching, shifting.

Alicia Hilton

Welcome to Draco Intergalactic Space Station

A. Hybrid human-machine, hacker, thief—when you fled Earth and your creator, the crypto that you stole bought you a new face and an apartment on Draco Intergalactic Space Station, a colony that protects all citizens from prosecution for past crimes committed on Earth.

Your condo is a cramped studio furnished with a single porthole window, a cot, two chairs bolted to the metal floor, and a small table, but living in a home that's the equivalent of a large metal box is a hell of a lot better than being hunted for your body parts. The AI that controls your brain is not superior to an UltraSynth android's operating system, but your mutated human heart, lungs, kidneys, and intestines have stronger rejuvenating powers than Valarnose Youth Elixir.

Fortunately, your new neighbors haven't tried to feast on your flesh, a miraculous feat of restraint because the dude who lives next to the laundry room is a Ravonvian who's had arachnid jaw and leg mods. Perhaps he assumes you're a homicidal fiend who's more dangerous than him? Your Moodhat often radiates red light, a clear indicator that you've got rage issues. Or maybe he fears that he will be jailed if he violates a DRACO EDICT?

DRACO EDICT #3 *Respect Feelings*—when a citizen's Moodhat indicates emotional turmoil, be kind and respectful.

During sixty-two days of coexisting with other criminals, you've settled into a dull routine—work, gym, eat, dose yourself with SomnumNu so you won't have nightmares when you sleep. By the end of each day you're exhausted, a draining fatigue you hope will dissipate when you finally feel safe.

After you clock out at the superconductor factory, you usually jog through the Transport Hub so you can see new arrivals disembark. Whenever you see a passenger with long black hair you do a double take, wondering if the woman might be Tilda, the scientist you once believed was your biological mother. She pretended to dote on you like a daughter but was raising you so she could harvest your organs. Is it loathing or a need for closure that makes you want to see Tilda again? Perhaps there's still a glimmer of love for her in your mutated heart.

Since New Year's Day is a holiday when shuttles don't operate, you take a shortcut through Park Biodome. The verdant interior mimics a pastoral scene from England, except there are no sheep or cattle. You see an elderly human woman sitting in the gazebo, cuddling a sentient plant on her lap.

The woman pats the Dogmint's fuzzy head and says, "Would you like a treat?" She pulls a bag of tofu cubes from her shirt pocket.

The jade-green shrub *yips* and wags its branches. *Yip, yip,* the Dogmint's leaves ruffle and spread apart. A mouth surrounded by glistening barbs opens wide.

"Be gentle," the woman says.

A tongue that looks remarkably like a dog's tongue darts out to receive the offering. As the shrub masticates, the tips of its leaves shimmer.

The woman also radiates joy. Her Moodhat changes in color from pale pink to fuchsia.

Your own Moodhat fades, the bright red beam turning a listless shade of sallow yellow.

You've never had a pet. Tilda did not have animals or sentient plants in the laboratory that was your home. When you escaped after drugging Tilda and hacking the security system, you encountered a stray dog on the street but didn't have the courage to touch it.

The Dogmint yips again and hops on the woman's lap, begging for another treat. She rewards it with two more tofu cubes.

You sniff, fighting the urge to weep. You've never felt such acute yearning for affection. Slowly, you walk towards the woman and the Dogmint.

The Dogmint tugs at its leash and squeals.

"You want to go home?" the elderly woman says. She puts the Dogmint in a carrier and glares at you.

"Sorry to intrude," you say. If you decide to visit the Botanical Bazaar to shop for a sentient plant companion, Proceed to **C.** If you leave the park and go straight to the gym, Proceed to **B.**

*

B. The gym is packed with gym rats—human-sized rodent extraterrestrials sprinting on the treadmills. You stride past the sweaty extraterrestrials and enter the cycle center. All the bikes are taken. You enter the weight room.

An Endoparasitoid Wasp is doing bicep curls. The big, armor-clad brute sees you and drops the dumbbells. "Need a spotter?" Her tongue darts out as she leers at you, ogling your body.

"No, thanks," you say. Even if you were attracted to Wasps, why would you date an Endoparasitoid? Their halitosis is horrendous.

You walk towards the bench press, but the Wasp is doggedly persistent. She follows you and says, "Sweet cheeks, you shouldn't work out alone. Wouldn't want you to get hurt." Her mandibles snap open and her secondary mouth juts forward. Slime drips from the fangs.

The Wasp is violating DRACO EDICT #1 *Respect Free Will*—do not use tech, mind control, or threats to manipulate fellow citizens.

You glance at the security camera that is mounted on the ceiling. The indicator light is illuminated, which means your encounter will be recorded if you press the red panic button on the wall.

The Wasp steps in front of the panic button and *clacks* her mandibles.

You grasp the taser that's in a holster strapped to your waist and say, "No means no. Back off." The weapon is set to stun. If you give the Wasp a zap, Proceed to **Z**. If the Wasp backs off and you leave the gym without wounding her, Proceed to **C**.

*

C. You catch the complimentary hovercraft shuttle to the Botanical Bazaar.

Two Lorastroons are sitting on the bench closest to the door, smooching. Slime oozes from their leech-like mouths. Fortunately, Lorastroons are not aggressive, but their amorous display makes you feel even more lonely.

You sit on the only vacant seat, next to a bald human who snores like a Bearzorian. He holds a tote bag on his lap that twitches and *chirps*. The bag isn't sheer, so you can't see whether his pet is a plant or a bird. The man must be content with his companion because his Moodhat radiates bright pink light.

A human with extraterrestrial augmentations is sitting across the aisle. She's wearing a miniskirt that's so short it barely covers her crotch, and her feline legs are impressively muscular. You wonder why she's not wearing a Moodhat, but you try not to stare.

The hovercraft *zooms* past the Financial District. Holograms project from buildings, advertising brokerage services. All the financial advisors in the ads wear pink Moodhats.

Your own Moodhat dims, the light changing to a shade of yellow so pale that it's almost ivory.

Finally, you see the Botanical Bazaar in the distance. Proceed to **D.**

*

D. The hovercraft latches onto the dome-shaped building, and the vehicle's door opens directly into a huge greenhouse. A recorded voice says, "You have arrived at the Botanical Bazaar."

The Lorastroons quit kissing and exit the shuttle. Other extraterrestrials and humans trundle past you in an orderly row, but the sleeping man next to you still snores. His long legs block the aisle.

You tap his shoulder and say, "Excuse me."

The bag on his lap wriggles and *chirps, chirps, chirps* until he wakes with a start. The man slings the tote bag over his shoulder and hurries towards the door.

As you sprint after him, your Moodhat radiates tangerine light.

The shuttle's recorded voice says, "Please stand clear of the closing doors. Next stop, Organ Extraction Emporium."

You leap from the vehicle as the doors are shutting. Proceed to **E.**

*

E. As you enter the greenhouse, your Commerce Wristband beeps as it synchs with the Botanical Bazaar's vending system. All commercial transactions, except for bartering, are done electronically, through wristbands or cranial implants. Since you haven't had mods, you must wear a wristband.

Your band glows yellow, indicating that the overdraft feature has been activated. You press a button on the side of the band and say, "Verify balance." Your monthly paycheck should've been deposited yesterday.

A Proboscidean alien wearing a green apron prances towards you. Proboscideans are bipeds with legs as stocky as elephants and long trunks. He raises his trunk and says, "Welcome to the Botanical Bazaar. May I help you?"

"When does the next shuttle arrive?" you say.

"In twenty-nine minutes. We're having a Dogmint sale. Can I show you some plants?"

"I'm just looking."

The hair on his head stiffens and starts twitching. "You'd be more comfortable with a human guide?" he says.

Embarrassment makes you blush. You raise your wristband. "I'm just looking."

He sees the band's yellow light and snorts, flapping his trunk. "Have a nice day," the Proboscidean says. He turns away and shuffles towards a Ventorlian arthropod extraterrestrial who's looking at a fertilizer display.

You glance at your wristband, hoping it will change color, but it still flashes yellow. There should be 439 Dracodollars in your crypto account. Working on the assembly line at the superconductor plant is sweaty drudgery, mind-numbing, but it was the only job available when you applied.

Scarlet light streams from your Moodhat. You're tempted to remove the glowing cap and crush it, but don't want to cause a scene. A second later, your crypto account balance is updated, and your wristband turns green. Proceed to **F.**

*

F. You walk down the central aisle. The dome's interior is more spacious than you expected. Since this is your first visit to the Botanical Bazaar, you are shocked by the cacophony of sounds. Thousands of trees, shrubs, bushes, and vines *yip*, *bark*, *chirp*, *giggle*, *sigh*, *hiss*, *snore*, and *growl*.

A voluptuous woman walks towards you. She's either human or an android—one of the UltraSynth models. She's wearing a rose-colored Moodhat and a skin-tight bodysuit that's the same shade of emerald as her eyes. The vine that's wrapped around her neck waves when she says, "Welcome to the Botanical Bazaar. What kind of companion are you looking for?"

Her voice is as soothing as her smile, and you're extremely relieved that the vine is not acting terrified. Your Moodhat flickers, fluctuating from red to lemon yellow to coral. You say, "I'm not sure. I've never had a pet plant."

"It's your first visit? Marvelous." She claps her hands. "May I suggest a fern? They're easy to care for."

If you agree to look at the ferns, Proceed to **H**. If you say, "I'd like to see the carnivorous plants," Proceed to **G**.

*

G. Your guide says, "Excellent choice. FelineThyme is very popular. We also have Flytraps and Bladderwort, if you're looking for a more exotic companion." She leads you down the center aisle.

You stroll towards two winged bipeds. At first, you assume the customers are Mothrane aliens because of their lacy forelimbs, but their faces are human—no insect mandibles or compound eyes. They must be humans with surgical modifications.

Envy makes you pause. Their augmented wings are impressive, but you're coveting their relationship—the couple wears matching harmony rings.

You've never had a lover or a friend. Until you escaped the laboratory, you'd never encountered any humans except Tilda.

The taller winged man strokes a flowering plant. He smiles when it *purrs*. The round bush is about the size of a grapefruit and has pointed leaves that are covered with orange fur.

The winged man's partner leans closer and kisses his cheek.

Your guide misinterprets your interest and says, "Those plants are Foxglove. They're friendly but aren't recommended for amateur botanists."

"Why?" you say.

"Fast propagation. They reproduce asexually and can have a litter of kits every twenty-eight days."

If you say, "They're adorable. I'd like a Foxglove," Proceed to **I**. If you say, "My apartment's too small for kits. Can I see the FelineThyme?" Proceed to **J**. If you say, "I'd like to see the ferns," Proceed to **H**.

*

H. Your guide says, "My first pet was a fern. She's almost ten and still frisky. Loves to play fetch. I take her with me when I jog."

Your Moodhat beams cantaloupe-colored light as you imagine a fern scampering around your apartment. "Do ferns need to be leashed?"

"Yes, they get skittish around strangers."

You're skittish around strangers, too. You feel affinity for the ferns. Shimmery salmon light radiates from your Moodhat.

Your guide turns left when you reach the next row of plants.

The ferns are an unpleasant shade of olive green speckled with brown, but they have lacy fronds that rustle. You say, "Is it okay if I touch them?"

"Move slowly," the guide says.

You select the shortest fern, a plant that's about three feet tall. When you stroke a frond, it twitches. The delicate membranes are softer than you expected. Since it does not appear to have a mouth, you say, "How do they eat and drink?"

"Ferns don't eat. Water their roots once a week. Place the plant next to your window."

If you say, "I'd like a plant that's more affectionate. I want a Foxglove," Proceed to **I**. If you say, "Could you show me the FelineThyme?" Proceed to **J**.

*

I. Your guide says, "Are you sure you want a Foxglove? We don't accept returns."

You say, "Ferns are too big. I'd like a smaller plant that has furry leaves, a pet that fits in my hand."

She leads you back towards the Foxgloves.

The winged men have left, but the obnoxious Proboscidean is watering a Foxglove that has peach-colored blossoms. He stops spraying water from his trunk and snorts. The rude noise makes your temper flare, and your Moodhat blinks and turns red.

Your guide says, "Harold, the Drakon Delphiniums are looking dry. Could you give them a quick mist?"

"Yes, Leena," the Proboscidean says. He lowers his trunk and shuffles towards an aisle on your right.

You want to introduce yourself to Leena, but shyness makes you tongue-tied.

Leena says, "What color of flower do you prefer?"

The tiny blossoms come in a kaleidoscope of colors—pastels and bright shades of yellow, pink, purple, green, and blue.

Leena's emerald-colored eyes are mesmerizing and inspire you to say, "Emerald green."

She searches the row, but none of the Foxgloves have emerald-colored flowers.

You consider requesting a plant that has violet flowers, but don't want to appear fickle. You say, "Can I touch them?"

"Avoid the buttocks," Leena says.

"How can you tell which end's the buttocks?" The short bushes are round and look the same on all sides.

Leena giggles. Her laugh is so delightful that you chuckle.

She picks up a plant that has pale green flowers. Most of the roots are spindly and dry, but one thicker root is covered with mucous. The Foxglove spreads its leaves open, displaying a puckered mouth, and *yips*. The lips are the same shade of pale pink as the mucous.

You start to feel queasy.

"Do you want to hold it?" Leena says. Before you can answer, she

ALICIA HILTON

plops it in your hand.

The furry leaves feel as soft as velvet, but the mucous is gooey and has a musky scent. If you say, "Can I see the Feline Thyme?" Proceed to **J**. If you pet the plant and say, "Darling, do you want to come home with me?" Proceed to **Y**.

*

J. Leena leads you down a wider aisle on the opposite side of the dome. Vents in the ceiling pump a blast of steam. The vapor makes you sweat, but you're enjoying Leena's company too much to leave. You approach a large sign that says—WARNING CARNIVOROUS PLANTS. The vine around Leena's neck *whimpers*.

Leena strides faster as you pass the Flytraps. Some of them are as tall as Giraffaliens.

The giant Flytraps thrash and *hiss, hiss, hiss, hissssss*. You stop to stare at one of the huge jungle plants. Thick, metal chains are wound around the trunk. The waxy, green leaves have bluish veins that remind you of human anatomy. The trunk pulses, like fluid is pumping through it.

"Does it have a heart?" you say.

"Two hearts," Leena says.

"Isn't it cruel to keep them chained? Shouldn't they be allowed to exercise?"

As if the plant understands your questions, it thrashes more vigorously. The kidney-shaped maw opens, lunges, and clamps around your head. Proceed to **K**.

*

K. You struggle and scream, but the Flytrap is so strong that it lifts you off the ground.

You draw your taser and press the trigger repeatedly, until the weapon won't fire again, but the shocks don't stun the Flytrap. Digestive enzymes seep into your skin. The burning sensation is horrific. The trap tightens further. Your will to live surges. With the last of your strength, you pummel the maw with your fists.

Suddenly, you're doused with a blast of warm water.

The carnivorous beast opens its trap to *hiss*, and you fall to the floor.

Leena grasps your hand and helps you to stand. The wet floor is slippery. You take a step and stumble.

More water sprays at the plant that attacked you. The Flytrap *roars*, but you're too terrified to turn around and look at what's happening.

Leena wraps her arm around your shoulder. Together, you hobble towards the FelineThyme. Proceed to **L**.

*

L. Your heart is pounding. You start seeing spots. Suddenly, you're overcome with dizziness. Proceed to **M**.

*

M. When you wake from being unconscious, Leena is using a towel to wipe your face. She says, "I'm so sorry! Are you okay?"

The vine around her neck *whines* and twitches.

Your head hurts, but you're so grateful to be alive that you whisper, "Yes. I'm okay." You try to stand, but you're so dizzy you collapse again. Proceed to **N**.

*

N. As you regain consciousness, a middle-aged man who you haven't seen before sprints towards you, with the Proboscidean shuffling at his side. The Proboscidean raises its trunk and sprays warm water at your face, washing away Flytrap digestive enzymes and your tears. Proceed to **O**.

*

O. You touch your head. Your Moodhat has fallen off. Your scalp is swollen but isn't bleeding.

Leena pats your shoulder. "Should I call an ambulance?"

The middle-aged man must be Leena's supervisor, because he says, "Leena, you're fired."

Leena says, "Don't blame me. I told you the Flytraps were dangerous!"

"You should've requested an escort," he says.

You say, "If you fire her, I'll report you for violating DRACO EDICT #2 *Respect bodily integrity*—when a citizen or their property commits a grievous assault the punishment is banishment."

Leena's boss says, "I apologize! Leena, you're not fired." Proceed to **P.**

*

P. When you sit up, your head throbs, but you don't see spots. Proceed to **Q.**

*

Q. The Proboscidean snorts and snorts again, but the rude noises make you smile.

"Thank you for saving me," you say.

The Proboscidean raises his trunk and douses you with more warm water.

Leena says, "Do you want us to call an ambulance?"

"I'd like to see the FelineThyme," you say. Proceed to **R.**

*

R. The Proboscidean wraps his trunk around your belly and tugs you to your feet.

You tremble and say, "Thank you. I can stand without help."

The extraterrestrial's wrinkled, leathery trunk has rough bristles, but you pat the trunk as it slithers off your belly.

Leena and the Proboscidean walk beside you, towards an aisle that's two rows over. As you approach the row of short, fuzzy shrubs, you hear *purring*. Proceed to **S**.

*

S. FelineThyme does not meow, but the *purring* is such a comforting sound.

"Can I touch them?" you say.

Leena says, "Yes, but avoid the tails. They like it when their ears are rubbed."

"Where are the ears?" You worry that she's going to lift a plant and show you a root that's coated in mucous, but Leena says, "You see the tallest fronds? Those are the ears."

The plant that you touch *purrs* louder and rubs against your hand.

The Proboscidean snorts, but the sound of his exhalation is higher pitched than before, as if he's mimicking the purring.

"She likes you," Leena says.

"The FelineThyme's a girl?"

"Yes, females have darker fur."

FelineThyme is everything that you'd hoped for in a pet. You say, "She's perfect. I'd like to take her home with me." Proceed to **T**.

*

T. Leena picks up your FelineThyme and says, "Follow us to the pet boutique. I'll wrap her up and give you a care sheet." Proceed to **U**.

*

U. The pet boutique is on the north side of the building. You're relieved that you don't have to walk past the Flytraps.

Leena points to a display of ribbons. "Bows are complimentary. What color would you like?"

Suddenly emboldened, you say, "Emerald. It'll remind me of your eyes."

The Proboscidean barks, a staccato sound that resembles a laugh.

ALICIA HILTON

Leena writes her phone number on top of the Pet Care Sheet and gives you three complimentary cans of Feline Savories. "Kitties prefer live food," she says. "If you let her roam, keep her on a leash so she doesn't run away when she's chasing cockroaches."

You wipe your wristband across the IdentiScanner.

Leena hands you the tote bag. Your kitty *purrs*. Proceed to **V.**

*

V. Your metal-clad apartment doesn't feel empty anymore, now that you have a FelineThyme. You open a can of Feline Savories. The mustard-colored gel smells like fish.

The FelineThyme's branches quiver. The center of the shrub opens, revealing a mouth that has pale green lips. The FelineThyme bends her head, a green tongue darts out, and she slurps up the gel. Minutes later, she's curled up on the end of your cot, rubbing against your feet. Her fuzzy branches vibrate as she *purrs*.

You look at your kitty and say, "Should I call Leena?"

The FelineThyme twitches her ears.

You pick up your smartphone.

Leena answers after the first ring. Maybe she's human, maybe she's an android, but whether blood flows through her veins doesn't matter. You've made a friend. Your Moodhat radiates shimmery pink light.

There is no **W** or **X**. **V** is the end of the story, unless you dare to visit **Y** or **Z**.

*

Y. You pay for your Foxglove and are waiting for the hovercraft shuttle to arrive so you can return to your apartment. A nine-foot-tall Xenomorph strides towards you, *thunk, thunk, thunk, thunk*. You try not to tremble when he ogles your pet carrier. His tongue darts out. "What'd ya get?" he says.

"Foxglove." You smile, but your stomach clenches. You hold your carrier tighter. It's vibrating, and you're worried that your Foxglove is frightened.

The Xenomorph peers into the carrier's mesh ventilation panel. "Hungry sweetie?" he hisses. The Xeno opens his fanny pack and pulls out a chunk of raw meat that's as big as your fist. "Let me feed 'em."

The Foxglove *chitters*.

Your taser isn't powerful enough to stun a Xeno, so you unzip the carrier's flap.

The Foxglove leaps from the carrier, launching itself at the raw meat. The plant's mouth opens wide, *wider*, exposing teeth so sharp they look like ivory-colored needles. The teeth tear into flesh.

You stagger back but aren't fast enough to avoid getting spattered by blood.

The Xeno strokes the Foxglove as it devours the meat. "Precious. *My* precious."

If you say, "Give me back my pet!" Proceed to **Z**. If you're too petrified to speak, flee to **H** and take refuge with the ferns!

*

Z. Angry Endoparasitoid extraterrestrials have appetites as voracious as their tempers. Challenging a sadistic, armored brute leads to a fate worse than death. Flee as fast you can, before the cretin lays eggs in your throat! Return to **C**!

ALICIA HILTON

Gemma Cooper-Novack

Notes and Sounds

I was singing up to the hollow rafters of a barn that made you think
it was older than it was. It was called the New Building and its outsides
were painted endlessly, white forms on black shadow. The notes
on the page were distinguished by shape but even in a normal format
I couldn't read music. Elka's thick freckled arm pounded a tempo out
of the air. I sang, figuring the tune out from listening to my section.
I was a soprano. I was seventeen. Vermont stretched above me, star-thick
sky. We sang without words first, stretching out sounds. I'd remember
the words twenty-two years later. I would have imagined a completely
different life twenty-two years later, but I wasn't thinking about it.
Someone had kissed me last night in the puppet museum, his dick
nudging my thigh, and I wanted it. This morning he'd groped me under
the dragon puppet during rehearsal and I'd slammed my upper arms
over his wrists, and he didn't stop. I wanted to sing now. Elka's arm sliced
the air and her foot stamped wide on the packed dirt floor. Everyone
in the barn was older than I was. All of them knew how to live. Elka's mother
was visiting from Russia. I'd talked to her on the porch in the morning
when hay across the road glowed and bright morning stars were rising
like in the song we were singing.

Gemma Cooper-Novack

The wrong stories

I always pick the wrong karaoke songs—I know the lyrics to creepy
ones, in my range when I sing them in the shower. It's one of the only
ways I get embarrassed. At the last bar I sat at indoors, a woman I
never kissed and I'm still not sure why I fell for gave her all to Alanis,
voice stopping the room like a lightning strike. Like Alanis, she made
the wrong syllables long, tongue unimaginably close to the mic. I
spent hours not running my fingers through her hair, imagining the
soft spiky crop against my palm. I drove her home and I never went
out again, just imagined her. Sex is the other way I get embarrassed,
absence deep as a canyon. Someone touched me the week before I went
inside, soft clothed bodies on her couch. I didn't recognize my weight.
Months later I was scared when we went hiking, unready for touch. She
brushed up against my soft spiky conversation. It didn't yield. Alone I
crave the contradiction of embrace and unyielding membranes, night
sheltered under covers, song that vibrates off the ceiling.

Joel Scarfe

Salting the Ocean

Something about the books,
their spines fading on a sunny shelf
and he is weeping again
for the wasted years, for the spilled drinks
and the suffering. The days move
faster now across the earth, and all of them
carrying a small box of sorrow
that no light will ever penetrate.

The love that put its delicate fingers in the heart
is defenceless. Its poor soft feet
will not help it along the broken glass
of the years. He weeps, and can't get it out
of his mind — that obdurate whale
swimming the globe in search
of a mate. Its huge lonely tears
salting the ocean.

William James Ó hÍomhair

Bealtaine na Briotáine

Seanfheirmeoir béal dorais
a stad muid ar an mbóthar
an 30ú lá de mhí Aibreáin

"Déanaigí anocht é, nó beidh sé ródheireanach"
fear ciúin, loighiciúil, praiticiúil, ina bhealach féin
a chroch craobhacha feá ar leac na fuinneoige
's nuair a d'fhiosraigh muid cad chuige, muid na stráinséirí óga,
go cúthalach, a dúirt sé, gurbh in a dhéanadh na seanóirí
nuair a bhí sé ina bhuachaill óg

agus deir sé nach labhraítear
teanga an bhuachalla sin,
a thuilleadh
go bhfuil dearmad déanta ag an seandream
agus neamháird ag an dream óg
is gur thug sé féin cúl léi
i bhfad ó shin
muise, cén tairbhe a bheadh inti?

ach nuair a fhiafraím, cé hiad na crainnte sin
atá chomh tábhachtach céanna,
"Faou" a deir sé, is deirim "feá"
"Derv" a deir sé, is "dair" a deirim

ag tiomáint abhaile dom,
an lá dar gcionn
trí bhailte agus trí shráideanna
b'fhacthas dom iliomad craobhacha
á gcrocadh sna fuinneoga
is ba ghlas iad fós na duilleoga

William James Ó hÍomhair

May in Brittany

An old farmer next door
stopped us on the road
on the 30th day of April

"Do it tonight, or it'll be too late"
A quiet, logical, practical man, in his own way
 hanging branches of beech on the windowsill
 and when we inquired about them, the young strangers we are,
 shyly, he said it's what the old people did
 when he was a young boy

And he says that the language of that boy
is not spoken
anymore,
 that it has been forgotten by the old,
 and never known by the young,
 and that he himself turned his back on it
 a long time ago
 sure, what use is in it?

but when I asked, what are these trees that
 are so important still,
 "Faou" he says, and I say "feá"
 "Derv" he says, "dair" I say back.

driving home
the next day
through towns and streets
I saw many branches
hanging in the windows
the leaves still green.

David Ishaya Osu

One suitcase

You came back home with a stalk of fresh memories, raw.
You came back with flowers. In the mirror of mind is a basket of gold.
A day stuck in rainstorms. You went out.
Far away from your 'hood. In the rain. In the mood. In time.

There is always beauty to behold, there is always a camera in your hand.
A zoom lens is your most preferred machine; you prefer to see from afar.
You prefer to love from afar. The farther the knowledge, the closer it
    gets to you.
This is one reason your eyes and ears do the job. Birds have theirs.

Understanding and misunderstanding happen in a distance. You thought
It was a dead leaf until you went closer and saw that it was
A living leaf covered by a dead leaf. A living thing took the shape of a
    dead leaf.
The same sky gives us light and darkness, you said; the same body carries
    life and death.

You would photograph each sight of wonder, each turn of magic, each
    bend of time. A touch,
A wink, a smile, a gasp, a thought, each moment stuck to your body like
    harmless bugs.
They reminded you of morning dews and trying to find a path
In the thickness of unlit dawn. Village days, city days, old and new.

You wanted to exhaust the time you had left, to explore the city and capture
Its dynamics. Home was calling you. You wanted to lay your eyes on
The new manners of your city. You wanted to leave with more than
One suitcase of memories: love, streets, flowers, scars, blue, bottles and
    timelessness

Maidhc Ó Maolmhuaidh

Eipeagram 12.18

Scríofa ag an bhfile Máirteal circa 102 AD

A Iúibheanail, a chara,
Fad a bhíonn tú ag spaisteoireacht i Subura callánach,
Nó ag satailt suas le himní cnoc an bhandé Diana,
Ag cur allais trí do thoga ag leac doirse móruaisle,
Mar fhánaí a bhí tuirsithe ag cnocáin na cathrach:
Bhí fáilte is féile romhamsa faoin tuaith
Théis iomaí na Nollag ag cathair Bhilbilis,
Is í maorga galánta le hiarann is ór.
Is anseo go leisciúil a thugann muid faoi
An obair gan stró, cuairt a thabhairt ar na tailte
Boterdus is Platea – logainmneacha borba
I dteanga na gCeilteach sa taobh seo na Spáinne –
Taitneamh a bhainim as codladh gan náire,
Ag fanacht sa leaba go dtí naoi a chlog,
An cúiteamh is cuí don chodladh a chailleas
Théis iomaí na hoíche, scór bliain is deich.
Ni aithnítear toga, ach gach uair a iarraim,
Tugtar dom balcais ón gcathaoir is gaire.
Ag éirí ar maidin, céard a chím os mo chomhair,
Ach adhmad sa tinteán ón doire máguaird,
Is potaí ar crochadh in aice an teallaigh,
A bhfuair bean an mhaoirseora mar mhaisiú don tí.
Bíonn sealgaire farat, ach an cineál sin duine,
A bheadh uait i do chóngar i gcoillte faoi rún.
Tá an maor tí ag déanamh soláthair do na gasúir,
Is iarrann go héadrom faoi bhearradh dá ngruaig.
Mar seo fearr an tsaoil. Mar seo d'fhéadfainn éag.

Maidhc Ó Maolmhuaidh

Epigram 12.18

While you are strolling in noisy Subura,
Or desperately treading the hill of the Goddess Diana,
Sweating through your toga on the doorsteps of nobles,
As a follower made weary by the hills of the city:
There was a welcome and a celebration before me in the country
After many Decembers at Bilbilis,
elegantly beautiful with iron and gold
This is where we lazily go about
work, paying visits to the lands of
Boterdus and Platea – gruff place names
from the Celtic language in this side of Spain –
I enjoy sleeping without shame,
Staying in bed until nine o'clock,
The most fitting redress for the lost sleep
of many nights, thirty years.
The toga is not known here, but when I ask,
I am given a rag from the nearest chair.
Rising in the morning, what do I see in front of me
but wood in the house from the surrounding thicket,
and pots hanging by the fireside
that the bailiff's wife has used to decorate the house.
The huntsman is next, the kind of person that
you would want on your path in hidden forests.
The bailiff gives the boys their rations,
and asks softly that they trim their hair.
Like this it pleases me to live. Like this I hope to die.

Barbara Lock

Rabbit

We pass a farm stand to the right of the highway past the intersection at Ridge Hill Road and then a low, flooded field where Canada geese paddle among floating grasses. A hill comes at us fast and hard; on its crest, a large, cast concrete head gazes down at the parkway traffic.

"Man in the mountain," says Pope, his voice cracking. He's behind me, in the passenger-side backseat of the minivan.

"Rabbit's coming," says Dennis, my husband. He leans forward against the steering column, watches the driver's side mirror. Cal, next to Pope, squirms against his seatbelt, twists toward the window. He pushes the hair out of his eyes, but it falls back again.

"What does that mean, 'rabbit'?" asks Cal.

"Count to ten," says Dennis.

"One, two," says Cal.

"I don't like the way that thing looked at me," says Pope.

"Three, four."

"What thing?" asks Dennis.

"Five, six."

"That giant head," says Pope.

"Seven, eight."

"It was staring right at me," says Pope. "It was talking into my head. It wanted me to do something, but I didn't want to do it."

"Nine, ten," says Cal, and then a low, black sports car with a loud, thrumming purr speeds past us on the left. Cal watches the car until it disappears around the curve, then peers into the stand of dense, young maples whizzing past. "I still don't see a rabbit," says Cal.

"What head?" asks Dennis. He changes lanes to chase the fast car, even though he's already going seventy-five.

"It's not really a head," says Pope. "More like a mind. A consciousness."

"What does it want you to do?" I ask.

"I don't know," says Pope. "But whatever it is, I don't want to do it."

On the side of the road, an orange safety cone lies flattened, mangled.

"Regatta, regatta, regatta," says Dennis.

"What's a regatta?" asks Cal.

"You've been to a few," says Dennis.

"No, I haven't," says Cal. "I don't even know what one is."

"It's the boat race," I say, and I turn around to pat him on the knee, but he's already shrinking away, rolling his eyes, and then we have maybe forty seconds of relative silence while my husband jockeys for position among a Jeep, a Subaru, and another Pilot.

"Wasn't Albany the capital of the United States?" asks Cal.

"No, New York City," I say. "Very briefly."

"New Amsterdam," says Dennis, and then, looking in the rear-view mirror, "Rabbit." He changes back to the middle lane.

"Why does he keep saying 'rabbit' all the time?" asks Cal.

"Is Washington D.C. a big city?" asks Pope.

"It's spread out," says Dennis, then he starts to cough. "Lot of coppers," he says. And then, "You need rabbits."

"What's going on with that sound?" asks Cal. "It's going *zshh*, *zshh*, *zshh*." He sings through his teeth.

"Go rabbit go," says Dennis. He taps his fingers on the steering wheel.

"That's the tire," says Pope. "The tire makes that sound when it hits that part of the road."

"How can you tell?" asks Cal.

"I know things," says Pope.

We approach an overpass from which a banner hangs, tied to the safety fence. Blue letters on a white field: *Stop White Replacement*.

"Lost our rabbit," says Dennis.

"Is Buffalo a big city?" asks Pope.

"Decent sized. Freezing cold," says Dennis.

"It has an NFL team," says Pope.

"Can I tell you something?" asks Cal. "Do you know the city Oakland? Does Oakland have an NBA team?"

"Oh, Columbus Ohio. It's the largest city without an NFL team or an NBA team. Population almost a million," says Pope.

"Rabbit's up there," says Dennis.

"You're going too fast," I say. "If you can keep it under 80, I would appreciate it."

"Mom, chillax," says Pope.

"I got a rabbit up there," says Dennis. "Albany on your left."

"So cool," says Cal. "Look at that one cool building in the middle. It looks like a candle," and I look to see which building interests Cal, but all I see is a tall, brutal, concrete structure that could be a prison tower.

"Not even a hundred thousand people," says Pope. "Ninety-six."

We pass a white truck hauling a fifteen-foot maple tree wrapped, roots-and-leaves. We're driving along the west side of the Hudson now. On the east side of the river, an abandoned, three-level paddleboat sits low in the water.

"I don't like this town at all," says Pope.

"Why don't you like it?" I ask.

"I don't like it," says Pope, and I feel it too, but I don't see anything objectionable except a buzzard that lands on top of a telephone pole. The buzzard, with its domed head and hunched, black shoulders, looks like Count Dracula.

"We're not going North. We're going West," says Cal.

"Glenn Falls," says Dennis, pointing to a green sign. "State Basketball Tournament, 1989," he says. And then, "We almost won."

"Vampires are real," says Pope. "But they have nothing to do with blood."

"Vampires have fangs," says Cal. "That's how you can tell them from regular people."

"Wrong," says Pope. "They have ginormous foreheads. Just big heads generally."

"Look at my forehead," says Dennis. He pushes his hair back with his right hand, but it's a silly gesture because he's almost bald in the middle there. "I could be a vampire," he says. He stares at himself in the rear-view mirror, makes bug eyes, grimaces.

"No shot," says Pope.

"You'd be a really good vampire, Dad," says Cal.

"You'd be terrible," says Pope. "All disorganized and wasteful."

"I vant to suck your blood," says Dennis in a raspy, vampire-sounding voice, as Pope shakes his head.

"Embarrassing," says Pope, and Dennis glowers at me in that way, so I turn around to face the backseat.

"Your father can do anything he sets his mind to," I say.

"Peace and love, Mom," says Pope, in a falsetto.

A guy on a loud motorcycle passes on the left and changes lanes in front of us, slows down. His overlarge black shirt tee billows in the highway wind, revealing the pale skin of his skinny back: a heavy, linked chain—a tattoo—wraps around his waist; above the chain, on the man's mid back, plumes of smoke rise from a skull.

"That's great," says Dennis. "Gonna comb your hair, brush your hair, buy yourself some tattoos and a Harley," he says. The man on the motorcycle takes the exit.

"Can you roll up the window please?" says Pope.

"Your mother is sick," says Dennis.

"I don't understand why you don't close the window," says Pope.

"You don't take care of your horses, that's what happens to you," says Dennis.

"I don't have any horses. No one here has ever had any horses," says Pope.

"That's great," says Dennis. "You gotta fight for what you want. You want it? Go get it!"

"I definitely don't want a horse," says Pope.

"I want a cat!" says Cal.

"Silence," I say.

"When are we getting to the lake?" asks Cal.

"I'm setting a timer," I say, pulling out my phone. "I don't want anybody to talk for fifteen minutes." And then nobody talks for almost six. The highway wind shakes the panes, and Pope's wrenches rattle in the plastic door pocket, and thim, thim, thim, goes the car on the pavement. A slight drop in pitch from behind—it's a loud motor. Soon, a low, red sports car passes us on the left.

"Rabbit," says Dennis.

It's not even eleven by the time we reach Saratoga Springs, so we stop at a state park and follow a wide asphalt path down a steep hill. At the bottom, a fiberglass bridge takes us over a small river. Cal and Pope run ahead, and though Dennis pauses briefly on the other side of the bridge to wait for me, he waves his hand in a gesture that says *you take your time*.

The sound of the water is a man smacking his lips. The submerged weed that clings to the edge of the riverbed looks like green dreadlocks. A scraggly willow shelters a killdeer—black stripes across her forehead, another stripe fastens her beak in place. On the other side of the bridge and along the river path, wide bluestone steps lead down past the trail mix of dandelions and pine seedlings to a marshland wet with frogs.

"Spring comes early up north," I say, but no one hears me.

I catch up to Dennis and the boys; Cal jumps from rock to rock in the rust-brown water, while Pope stands on a boulder, arms crossed. I can't tell if he's looking at something up above the treetops, or if it's a thought that has his attention.

"Put your shoes on," says Dennis to Cal.

"Look," says Pope. "Look at the color of the rocks and the sand."

"That's iron," I say.

"Eye-ron," says Pope. "What's the deal with iron?"

"Big and strong," says Dennis. He flexes his pecs. "Be big and strong, Pope—like ox," he says, and "last one to the car is a loser." Cal runs over, tags Pope on the shoulder, and runs off down the trail loop back toward the car. My husband jogs after Cal, but I can see that he stops to walk after only twenty yards, and he holds his right hand to his chest. Pope stares at me.

"I'm waiting," says Pope. "For you to tell me about the water."

"Iron is a mineral required for the formation of hemoglobin," I say. "Blood."

"What happens when the water has a lot of iron?" asks Pope.

"To an entire city?" I wave my arms in a wide circle. "I'm not sure," I say.

"A whole metropolis," says Pope. He nods, strokes his scraggly chin hairs. Then he hops down from his rock and runs, slow and stiff-legged, up the path after his brother and father.

I notice the wind, a zephyr, which feels to me to be a color, a pinkish purple, lighter than your average magenta, more like dark peony. When I close my eyes, the color becomes richer, saturates, divides itself into a circular pattern of clustered red cells. A gust transforms the air into grape. And I think then that the wind must be visible to birds. That birds must see the air the way we see the ground. A set of sensors triggered by ruffled feathers that paints colors in the minds of flighted creatures. An airscape.

"I want a sky that imitates happiness," I say to no one in particular, and suddenly I recall that, recently, my teacher's son died in his sleep. I shiver.

Back in the car, silence.

"Did I tell you that my professor's adult son died?" I ask.

"Yes," says Dennis.

"He was my age," I say. Dennis starts the car, drives up the hill past the newly built condominiums and empty lots. Pope and Cal stare out the window. A pair of giant excavators, abandoned on the side of the road and drooping thick, steel cables, face each other as if to arm wrestle. "Why so quiet?" I ask. Dennis sighs and turns left past an open-air pavilion with a public faucet in the center. *Old Red Spring*, reads the hand-painted sign. "Pope, what happened?" I ask.

"It wasn't very nice, Mom," says Cal. Cal's eyes are moist.

"Your children aren't go-getters," says Dennis.

"What do you want them to go get?" I ask.

"I thought of another slogan," says Pope. "Saratoga Springs—our water tastes like blood."

"You come up here to win the race, you win the race," says Dennis, and Cal turns his head even more, so that he's almost looking backward, straining against the seatbelt.

"It's not today, is it?" I ask briskly. I turn to Pope.

"Tomorrow. I have to be there at eight," says Pope. "The time trials are at ten and the race is after lunch."

"Let's go carbo load," I say.

"No," says Dennis. "He needs meat. Meat will make him big and strong."

After we park, we see a white woman wearing a white dress, wig, and horns. A long-limbed woman who wears a red superhero unitard and a long, purple wig runs toward the angel-devil, but I can't tell if the two women are together.

"No parking anytime? What does that mean?" asks Dennis.

"That means no parking anytime," I say.

We park in front of an Irish bar and a smoke shop that sells edibles and pretty glass pipes.

In line in front of the restaurant, a woman says, "God forbid something should happen," and I wonder what she's talking about. In another party, four women in their twenties, each wearing a black sash inscribed with gold writing, cluster around each other, grab shoulders.

"God forbid we should eat at a different restaurant this time," says Pope. Cal hops on one foot, then the other, then he hangs onto the portable, fake iron railing that separates the line from the outdoor diners, and falls over, hitting his head on the fuzzy green mat on the concrete. "Get up," says Pope. Cal tries not to cry. I stand there with my arms crossed, while my husband pushes his way to the front of the line. "You're embarrassing," says Pope.

At the table inside, Dennis tries to order for me, but I don't want meat, and I contradict him to the waiter. Pope orders two meals.

"How come everything here looks the same?" asks Cal. I rub the back of his head, and he twists away, scowls, looks at the ceiling; the thin, metal I-beams that support the planked ceiling are a dull bronze. The large, cylindrical ceiling fixtures are wrapped in a synthetic, braided, bronze fabric. The floors, an unstained, unvarnished oak. I excuse myself to go find the bathroom. As I move among the tables, I notice that each seats a white family with hair that ranges in color from ash blond to medium brown. In the bathroom, dull, modern, bronze faucets emerge from dull, textured, bronze wallpaper.

When I get back to the table, everyone is eating tacos. Cal flashes a smile. "I vaguely think I've been here before," he says.

"That's called déjà vu," I say.

"I know," says Cal, triumphantly.

"You have been here before," says Pope.

"Why does everyone keep saying that to me?" asks Cal.

No one in the restaurant, which seats about 80 people, is a person of color, and I want to say this to my family, but I stay quiet. Pope pokes me in the shoulder and points to the table between ours and the bar, where the biceps of a bearded, bald man in a too-small tee busts forth from under his left cuff. There, in a tattoo, a clenched fist brandishes a knife. Behind the bar, several rows of large red, yellow, and green ceramic skulls glower at us.

"If you had to get a tattoo, what would you get?" asks Dennis.

"If I had to?" asks Cal. "A small dot," he says.

"I'd like to drink out of a cranium," says Pope. Dennis taps Pope's plate. "It's so spicy," says Pope, shaking his head.

"Twenty dollars, you eat the taco," says Dennis, and he starts coughing, but this time it doesn't stop for nearly two minutes, and a stocky server with close-cropped light brown hair and a goatee refills his waterglass.

By two o'clock, we are walking down the avenue, but I am a half-block behind.

"Mom!" shouts Pope. "Did you know that slow walkers are predisposed to dementia?" he asks. I give Pope a thumbs up.

A teen in a furry, blue, shark-like costume walks down the street with their parents, followed by a young man in a yellow Yu-Gi-Oh hood that ties beneath his chin. Then: two female samurai with primary-colored hair and plastic swords strapped to their backs; a woman in a pale pink dress with a tall ship tattooed on her left shoulder; a person in a full Spiderman morpho.

My phone buzzes—Dennis' text: *mountain company keep walking*.

On a side street, a bald, white, goateed man, this one wearing a black Mandalorean tee, steps aside to let me pass, even though there is plenty of room on the sidewalk. On the man's left calf, a tattoo: the word "Infidels." In the word, the middle "i" has been replaced by a silhouette of the Statue of Liberty.

I text Dennis: *Are you on the main street?*

A man in full sinister-clown makeup, complete with dyed green hair and a red, linen suit, lopes past.

I text Dennis: *Where are you?*

A woman in a Little Miss Muffet outfit—or could she be Little Bo Peep?—a light blue dress with white ruffles, walks as if her feet hurt.

Dennis texts me: *car.*

"I haven't seen any Black people in this entire town," I say, when I find them.

"Zero. Not a one," says Dennis.

"I saw one," says Pope. "In the restaurant."

"I like this place," I say. "But it's the whitest place I've ever been. Whiter than Florida."

"Well, it is," says Dennis.

"I don't feel good about that."

"You don't feel good about anything anymore."

"Can we go to the hotel now?" asks Cal.

"I'm not sick," I say.

"Okay," says Dennis.

"I just notice things," I say. "I notice when things are alive and when they are dead. Or mostly alive and mostly dead."

"Okay," says Dennis.

"Peace and love," says Pope, in falsetto.

"My teacher, the one whose son just died, he sent me an article about spirit, about Qi," I say. "The article says that when enough Qi accumulates, something is born. And when enough Qi has dissipated, something dies," I say.

"Got it," says Dennis.

"No, I don't think he's listening," says Cal.

We drive to the hotel. There's some talk about who gets what bed. Pope finds his crew in the lobby. I take Cal to the pool. But I can't form memory for a couple of hours, and I know the reason why, generally, even though I don't find out the details until much later: I ask for time alone, but I don't get it because my children need me, says Dennis. I have a duty, says Dennis. I fulfill a variety of duties and there is an evening meal involved and the satisfaction of other appetites.

Before bed, I read on social media:

The 18 yo yt man who shot
& killed 11 Black 2 yt in a
grocery store subscribed to the
Great Replacement conspiracy

"Dennis," I say.

"Don't read that garbage," he says. "It'll make you sad again." He goes to the window and draws the shade.

"It's connected," I say.

"You can't meditate your way out of everything," says Dennis. "You have to win, that's all. Make your kids the best they can be. So they can survive."

"That's not the way," I say.

Pope peeks around the door from the bathroom. He's rib-skinny, wet, nonchalant. "Towel?" he asks. Dennis finds a damp white towel on the light brown rug at the foot of the second bed and throws it at Pope, who doesn't catch it, lets it drop to the tile floor. Pope closes the bathroom door.

"Take your son," Dennis hisses. "Is he special? Most days he doesn't even try."

"You're asking the wrong question," I say.

"Yeah, tell me what I meant to say," says Dennis.

"You put too much stock in personal effort."

"Play to win, my father always said."

"What if the boys are not special in the way you want them to be special, is what you meant to say."

"That's what I did say," says Dennis.

Pope bursts into the room wearing a blue tee and knit boxers. His dark, wet hair hangs in large curls just below his chin.

"Big day tomorrow," says Dennis.

"My father's workshop was the most amazing place," says Pope in falsetto. "My father could make things with his hands that nobody else could make. He was a miracle worker, and he's the reason I am the man I am today," says Pope.

Cal rushes in from the adjoining room. "What's he doing?" he asks.

"The cars my father worked on weren't like anything else," Pope continues in falsetto. "When he drove those sports cars, he was immediately interesting, and unusual. I remember we took the Porsche ..."

"Pope," I say.

"Some of the happiest days of my life were driving with my father. My father and I drove home from Burlington, Vermont, back from a basketball tournament. Back roads. We had the Targa off, and we were trading places with a pair of motorcycles. I think they were Ninjas— crotch rockets."

"Who are you talking about?" asks Dennis, then he starts to cough, and he doesn't stop, so Pope raises his voice.

"The two motorcyclists were both wearing tee shirts. It was probably August. They definitely were wearing helmets, but there was this intense contrast between the severe danger of the tee shirt and the helmet," says Pope, still high-pitched.

"Where'd you hear all that?" asks Dennis, catching his breath.

"From you, Dad," says Pope, back in his normal, deep voice. Eyebrows raised. "Back when you had a vocabulary."

"I don't remember," says Dennis, and starts coughing again.

"But now you're all like 'Rabbit, rabbit. Strong like ox. Regatta, regatta, regatta.'"

"That's a compound sentence," says Dennis.

"No, Dad, it's not."

"Well, it's a complicated sentence," says Dennis.

"Nope," says Pope.

"Look, all I'm asking is that you try, Pope. Try to win. What I'm saying is, do you want to be the rabbit, or do you want to be the guy who chases the rabbit?"

"I'm done," says Pope, and he pulls on shorts and shoes and walks out of the hotel room without the key or his phone. Dennis makes a big show of going to the door and shouting, *get back in here or I'm through with you*, but he doesn't mean it. Nobody thinks he means anything by it, but what I can't figure out is who the performance is for. Pope ambles down the bronze-carpeted hall to the hotel stairs, and if he goes up or down, I never find out. I don't bother to look for him. I don't worry about him at all. I don't make any calls or text anyone, and when Cal asks if Pope is coming back, I tell him that Pope will either come back or he won't and in either case it will be for the best. Cal nods in agreement. Dennis glares at me and wanders around the hotel and then the city's main drag for who knows how long.

The next morning, Pope's crew clothes are missing and so is Dennis. At breakfast in the hotel lobby, I eat an omelet, while Cal goes for oatmeal with brown sugar.

"What does Dad mean when he says 'rabbit' all the time?" asks Cal.

"I know what, but I'm not going to explain it to you," I say.

"Okay," says Cal. And then he says, "I like rabbits. Sometimes I chase after rabbits in the park." His eyes get a faraway look and point up and to the left. "One time I was in the park with Dylan and we both saw a rabbit and it was very, very still and we both snuck up to it, moving so quietly, like we were predators. And we were going to get the rabbit, but then Dylan made a stupid move with his elbow, and then the rabbit hopped away, but like, really fast."

"I see," I say.

"I could have caught it though," says Cal. "I'm the fastest boy in my grade."

Susan Bruce

Splash Notes

How little I know.

One wave is a pile of sneezing cats that obey wind, rather than moon.
One wave gives up in fear and hands itself over to wet Jesus.
One wave looks like end-of-life for such a small thing that spirals.
One wave with a sinking feeling, falls into whales.
One wave is pecked by ghosts of rain.
One wave is a yellow room that turns all the lights on.
One wave believes in nothing but insists on enthusiasm.
One wave is the likeness of a too high rocket ship looking down.
Many waves hate to be touched.
Many waves are siblings every morning.
Many waves have a craving to roam rotten piers without invitation.
One wave is the great-great-grandwave of Hurricane Sandy.
One wave dreams of getting out of her portable basket.
One wave pumps its legs really hard to feel free.
Waves are extracted and rewoven to look out for one another.

Certainly, something is wrong with the spray of a splash
coming from the mouth of a highway.

Susan Bruce

Everything Is a Big Deal for an Ocean

1

I could lie around in a coma on an old mattress
surrounded by used tissues
capable of undeniable self-expression
that cannot express what I mean
because I don't know what I mean
and nobody tells me anything anymore.
I am divided into visitors that act like wolves.
I repeat I repeat I repeat like late-night television.
Over and over the drifts become do-overs.
And, I have so many giant boobs
I can't watch the ground closely. Everybody
knows how mixed up this is.
I finish nothing.
So, how do I think about me?

2

The storm is a tough neighborhood,
the sun with its eyes poked out.
I fall out of bounds. Wind is thrown around
at eighty miles an hour, as an aphrodisiac
making lots of noise as in hahahahahaha
hahahahahahahahahahaha.

Forthwith I climb flights of one hundred and sixty
stairs up to the white flag of sky, bargaining, exhausted
all at once. My cells separate into clementine seaweeds.
My body last remembers performing a handstand
before falling apart into a blaze of many concerns.

It's hard to believe the moon just sits there
as if for the first time, and if the moon can act
with such demeanor, such recalcitrance, then what?
I worry I should worry the sun will pilfer from me.

3

I live like a soft plaything.
The storm gutters
in my bed of sand.
I have no thinking
in accordance with
my tongue.
Reality is
a continuing
crystal current.
I am pushed
and cartwheeling
with all my silver parts
boneless jellies
fish with swords
fish with stars
fish with sails
and a smaller wave
inside me
bringing a glow
to daybreak.

Agnieszka Filipek

Działka

Dalie znów kwitną. Słoneczniki
pną się do nieba, a winogrona zwieszają się
ciężko. Każdy kogo spotkam, wciąż wspomina twoje

wino. Króliki są zabite, oprócz jednego,
który uciekł na siąsiednią działkę
i pozwoliłam im go zatrzymać. Czarna samica,

która miała młode zeszłego lata. Chwyciłeś maleńkie
stworzenie swoją białą papierową dłonią i dałeś mi
do potrzymania. Czułam na palcach bicie jego serca.

Agnieszka Filipek

Allotment

The dahlias are in bloom again. The sunflowers
stretch towards the sky and the grapes hang
heavily. Everyone I meet still mentions your

wine. The rabbits are killed, apart from one,
who escaped to the next door allotment
and I let them keep it. The black female

that had young last summer. You grabbed a tiny
creature with your white paper hand for me to
hold. I could feel its heartbeat on my fingers.

Jason Kennealy

Nettle

The sleeping's been up on blocks about a year now. Once that's out of whack, everything goes. You never get used to it – you're hoisted through your days on a meat hook, pretending you're awake only waiting to be lowered back into your queen-size casket to pretend to be asleep.

The doctor told me I should wind down before bed. Go carve out a routine for myself, get some exercise that isn't masturbation or petting the dog bald. I tried the cow's milk. The fancy one where they squeeze it out of them while they're looking at the moon. That's money I won't see again.

I caved and let them prescribe me a handful of fuck-knows-what. Not for me – you're rolling around in your sweat, somewhere between a coma and death. Your blood turns to tar in the pipe. Once morning comes, you're spat out the other end feeling stale and no better for it.

The house is perched on the coast of Duncannon. It's not much for size, but there are worse things to fall into your lap. The view is straight out of a giftshop, and I can heat the place for an hour by making a cup of tea and toast. I've three rooms – none of them work. I've made a go at luring sleep into the walls of each one.

It used to be that if there was a bullfight at the end of our bed, I'd carry on snoring. Now I'm lucky if I can nod off in the armchair for an hour – anything resembling a dream's gone as well. Snatches of them dangle in front of me and I've only the fire for company. And the dog – you should see her, a four-year old Kerry beagle. A rescue – she's afraid of birds and licks the armchair like it's sweets, but the body of a dog half her age. One look at her and you'd know she's worth something. She'd want to be, we endured three buses towards Donegal to pick her up.

I didn't even want her, but she made Morna happy. She wanted to name the thing after herself – said it'd be funny. I'm glad I talked her down off that one and we settled on Nettle or I'd be in a heap every time I called her for dinner.

My father loved the two of them. Whenever that toothless bogman would invite himself up to the house, he'd park his belly on the tablecloth, inhaling whatever cheap wine we had and I'd be listening to *my girls* this and that. Then, when he eventually toppled home, I'd throw the knife and fork he'd used into the sea.

Since what happened, the closest I've gotten to sleep was the bit of drink. A half bottle a night would get me about four hours of the stuff. It wasn't what I'm after – it only turned the thoughts inside me. I'd to pack it in, anyway, after I kicked the dog around the place one night. I came home to find her after making a nest of Morna's robe. I nearly killed her – I wanted to.

She's been cagey since, and she'll be a pile of bones and a bandana before she gives the paw again, but no doubt she'll live long enough to forget me. I leave her to it now, the scent's gone anyway and it's the only place she'll sleep.

The thoughts I have lapping around are never long landing in with her – Morna. The tiny frame of her, branded into my head. Sideways on the lino. Trembling in nothing but her skin by the fire.

It was late September. Summer's dying breath was on our necks. I spent the afternoon watching her paint and we said we'd chance a dip at the cove. It was going to be our last before the weather turned to dirt – I never enjoyed swimming alone and she wasn't built for the cold.

The swell was a bit rough, but she waded out, jumping through the waves. I watched from the shore as she dived under. She came up, her lovely ash-gray hair, stiff with salt from the day before, melted loose, trailing behind her like a dog fawning over its owner.

I followed her in and caught up with her. We separated, kicking water at each other, dunking our heads. I started swimming towards a small island. I looked back. I still don't know if it was a cramp or an undertow that ripped the feet out from under her, but she was down long enough. When she eventually came up, I booted it towards her.

I pulled her onto the sand. She coughed up a small child worth of sea water. I got her up to the house, undressed her and filled her with tea. She couldn't get a word out other than to convince me not to get a doctor. "I don't want to be a hassle," she said. That's how she spun it anyway, the state she was in – what's worse is I listened to her.

She lay down by the flame as her togs dripped dry beside her, before moving to our room. She slept until the next afternoon. She woke up a scrap of herself in the bed, and I was no better. She couldn't keep a boiled egg down and I'd to change the bed sheets with the sweat out of her, but she still refused a doctor.

We've a very old saying in Duncannon:

What's coming next is much worse.

The next day, I woke up to find her cold beside me. Something called delayed drowning. I'd never even heard of it. Easily preventable, I was told.

I slept through it.

I lay there with her and the dog until it got dark. I didn't open the curtains for a month.

Tonight, sleep is the usual foreign concept. A soup I had four days in the pot is burning a hole in my stomach. I'm tunneling my way through another bottomless night without a match. Nettle's curled beside me tail-twitching and I'm convinced the birdsong is taunting me.

I decide I'm getting up. The bed is as comfy as a heel of bread and I'll rip my skin off the bone if I spend another second on the thing. I haven't just become a smoldering pile of aspiration. I'm not about to drag my fingers through my hair, scrub the teeth with a wire brush and wring the day dry, but the nights have been at me long enough to know when to give up.

I sit up and plant my feet. I empty a bag of coal on the embers and boil up a carton of eggs. I suck on one in the heat of the living room. Morna's paintings stare back at me. The house is quiet – I've recently plugged the phone back into the wall – it's more ornamental than anything, but I suppose I'll have to back down on this self-imposed exile at some point.

I leave the fire bubbling and throw on the coat-and-wellie combo. I'm not sure of the time, but everything's a gray-blue. As I crunch down the garden towards the gate, I can hear the gulls diving at early shoals.

A first-light stroll is always good for getting me out of myself, breaking up the day and taking the wheels off the odd ideation. I walk the path that's reclaimed during the colder months along the cliff towards the cove.

I pick at whatever winter flower I can on the steps down to the beach. Old railway sleepers bet into the soil – ninety-eight of them. Seabirds nest in the holes where salt's eaten through. I get to the cove – I haven't been here in fucken ages. A year. The memories, even when it's warm, are rough.

I was only a pup. A boyish twenty-two without a hair on my chin. I'd noticed her down here collecting driftwood and being lovely. I said nothing, just watched her all day. I got about a month out of that until she introduced herself. That was that. I'd a full dose. I refused to move through the same world as her without trying it. That was in the spring, we'd each other under the hard spell and all by May.

It was mad. One of those summer-induced loves that'd haunt you forever – we were welded at the lips and the moths were going mad in my stomach. I'd a constant pain in my face from the laughing and cramps in my hand from all the holding. We jumped each other every chance we got – that potent, two mile an hour forehead-to-forehead type of stuff that'd wedge your soul open.

What a fucken waste.

That was then – when everything just fell into place and worked as it should. Now the effects of the world are at work and there's not even the fumes of her left. The wound's still fresh, but when you're three days on the trot without a wink the memory of her seems entirely false.

Just a few more winters and it'll be off to oblivion.

I stand in the shoreline, in the salt, below the rim of the wellies. There's a nip of fog around me. A giant's step away, an island looms, rising out of the water like the back of a waking animal. There's a boat sitting belly-up on the beach. I leave the flowers on the sand and wade back through the surf and flip it over. It creaks onto its hull and the oars fall out. I push it out before hopping in. I sever the rope.

My gaze spreads across the murk as I drift out through the last of the dark. My fingers are seizing around the oars. I can hear them before I see them – noisy blotches of fat anchored on the rocks. The sun peels back the night, brushing a bit of colour into the world, and I get a look at them. Seals – shining as their fat heads turn to look.

It must be the boat rocking, sleep almost takes me there and then, like some cruel voodoo. My jaw sags and I drop an oar. A slow blink of what feels like peace. I don't fight it. I almost go until the nose of the boat hits a rock and knocks it out of me.

I reach the island, maneuvering through the rocks. The belly of the boat wedges into the shore. I step out and my wellie fills. The tangles of seaweed grab at me as I wade onto the shale. The place is just jagged rock sat in cold fog. The trees are dead and hunched white with salt and Wexford is another life.

I float through an hour sitting on the stones, picking at a boiled egg. I'm far enough away to watch the seals eat. The big ones climb from the water, sand eel flapping in their mouths after a hunt and the pups chirping.

On the scent of the eggs, one of the bigger ones approaches – only looking. A pup slides out of their mother's folds. I jump back to put a bit of space between us. I turn and my foot snags between two rocks. It makes a sound and I drop.

I slide it out of the wellie. The skin's intact, but my ankle's after ripping clean of the socket. It flaps like a fish, a cartoon, but it's so cold I can only watch the pain.

I watch the tide turn and tug the boat from the gravel. It comes loose and floats out to sea. The fog clots around it as it bobs away. I just watch it go – the cold has me pinned. I'm stuck here. Stranded. Fucken moored on this rock and I could scream absolute misery until my throat swells shut and no one would know. I could chance the swim. I'd probably get halfway before my muscles twist and I fill with water – a fishing boat would pull me up in a net two days later.

I don't want to be a hassle.

The seals howl through the fog as it falls around me. The cold's hardened my skin. The feeling in my feet has completely gone. I unpeel an egg, shard by shard, and have another and another until my hands stop. A pup finds me in the mist, sniffing and squeaking at me, sticking its nose in my pocket. I hear the mother barking at him to get back. I can't move. She's going mad.

JASON KENNEALY

I could just leave her rip me apart, let her tear lumps out of me and feed the colony for the morning, but I throw the egg like a grenade. It lures the little fella back into the cloud and the mother's happy.

I pull my knees into my coat and decide to let the cold finish me. I think of Morna and Nettle – no better thought to see me out. The aftertaste of it all. What's left to me – the hollow space the size of her, and the dog, alone, wrapped around herself by the fire.

The spokes start turning.

The fire.

The thing's probably still roarin'.

I bite down on a piece of driftwood and pull my foot in its normal direction. It makes a noise and turns a similar shade of blue as the rest of me. I crawl in the direction I threw the egg. It's at the bottom of a rockpool being fought over by crabs. I don't unwrap it, I just push it into my mouth.

I crawl on my belly towards the shore, dribbling yolk. The sea's calm. It's not the swim that'll kill me, it's the hundred step climb soaked to the bone, but I'll chance it – the dog'll need feeding and there hasn't been a knock on the door in six months.

I take my socks off with my teeth, step out of my trousers and wade into the water. The ocean takes some of my weight and the waves help. I'm up to my waist. I dive under. I don't think, I can't – I just point myself into the fog and go.

My loose foot acts like a flipper. My body is like lead, but I'm moving forward. I'm swallowing water. I go under again and kick. My head is completely numb as I surface, the Wexford coast steps out of the fog. Salt scratches my eyes. Eventually the seabed snags my toes and strands of blood spread through the shallows as I emerge. The surge pushes me onto the beach. I drop to my knees, fold onto my face and cough up what I can.

The air hits my skin and freezes me in place. I force my eyes open, I'm looking at the steps. All ninety-eight of them. I get up another lungful of water and keep going. The steps are agony. I can't feel my body. The toes are as good as gone, but I make it.

I open the door and fall in a heap. I knock the phone off the wall as I scratch my way towards the fire. Nettle's doing her happy circles and starts licking the salt off my ears. I feel the blood sliding through my veins. My testicles nearly climb up my throat like a starved parasite. The fire thaws my spine and my bones uncurl in the flame. I close my eyes. It's like I'm being pulled under – the world backs away as sleep comes at me. I open my eyes as the sun moves in through the window and butters the cracks of my face. I smell the robe pressed to my nose and remember where I am. The phone's dial tone sings its dull note. Nettle's quiet beside me. I put my hand out and she lays her head across my chest. The fire's embers keep going, tipping along, under white ash.

Anna Teresa Slater

Morning Ritual

I pluck moringa off their
stems, one by one, forefinger
and thumb pressed

together in prayer, leaf
by trembling leaf. I hum
along with the soil, sun,

rain packed within its papery
green, each tug soft
magic. I am young again

and my father is teaching me
how to part clouds with
my mind, how to find the best

parking spot, how to hug
with my soul. I pick up another
iron-packed twig, gather

these forest teardrops into my
chipped bowl, I pull and I am
younger, overflowing, dangling

from a crackling tree. My father
at the other end of the street
lets go of the yellow dragon

kite and upside down I reach out
my arms as he flies toward me
in greatness. The weightless

mound grows yet remains
too small to cradle my heavy
head. Instead, I glide

my hand through the heart
of this silky hill. The feathery
cascade slips through

my fingers, settling into an airy
mantle as though they
understand the nature

of belonging. With touch
barely there, with roots digging
deeper somewhere far away.

ANNA TERESA SLATER

Alicia Byrne Keane

Making an Escape

Swimming, I see what my mother
would call a money spider
stalled on the ocean surface:
incongruity flickers, an awareness
of my own drifting hair. Later,
I can't remember if a scrap buoyed
the bead and tangle of its shape:
a leaf-fragment darkened by water,
some part of the undergrowth
detached to float and swirl.
I look up 'raft spider', find large,
inflatable-looking creatures; a 'sea spider'
is a centreless thing, all zigzag and crimp.
Nothing matches what I saw, so I re-learn
the shadows, tilted sepia: the hollow
between two waves, my hands
stubborn with cold.

Athira Unni

Postcard from England

We have crossed the sea now to live in
the coloniser's island. Labels of heaven,
hell, purgatory: irrelevant in a fresh plump
marriage. Uneventful days. I see a thistle
roll across the savage, somnolent moors.

At a distance, an octopus church stands
under clouds like grey puffy sugar candy.
In the gloom of waiting next to graves,
it stretches its tentacles along the streets.
The berried trees and driveways stir

and a bright red post-van disappears.
I think of my grandfather, his stamps,
the retired postmaster of his village
stretched out on his odorous old bed.
An old woman sneezes, keeps walking.

English has its poised lilts that scorn me.
Fish and chips and curry and baked beans
become recipes. My dowdy oven knows some
embarrassing secrets of burnt Sunday roasts.
Tickets booked. But we never go back home.

Trains arrive, depart. The sea is home-turf.
Its rules are simple: wave hello, goodbye.
It frames all: the sun, a boat, arrival, our life.
At a castle by the sea, a little boy runs, laughs
and falls to his knees, the rocks still and wise.

Amano Miura

Idir dhá réimse

Ní planda dúchasach mé –
Ní éiroidh leat ag iarraidh mé a aithint
I leabhar luibhealaíocht
Nó trí aip intleachtach shaorga.

Is neach hibrideach mé –
Meascán caithne agus céadair
Cumasc bambú agus neantóige
Leigheas aisteach is léir.

Ólam báisteach bhog fhionnuar
Cothaíonn Bainne na Bóinne mé,
Fásim i bhfoinse na talún
Cosnaíonn deora Amaterasu mé.

Bíonn rath orm sa ghort ríse –
Ach ní féidir liom fanacht
Toisc go bhfuil mo shíolta scapaithe freisin
Amuigh ar an bportach.

An mothaíonn tú an teannas seo idir dhá réimse,
Ag bogadh go brách i modh na sí?
Ní gheobhaidh tú mo fhréamhacha faoi thalamh in aon chor
Ach i mBealach na Bó Finne atáim i mo luí.

Amano Miura

Between two regions

I am not a native plant –
You won't identify me
In a botany book
or a free A.I. app.

I am a hybrid life form –
A mix of arbutus and cedar
A blend of bamboo and nettle
A strange tincture it seems.

I drink the soft, cool rain
The milk of Boann nourishes me,
I grow in the earth's hot springs
The tears of Amaterasu protect me.

I thrive in the paddy field –
but here I cannot stay
as my seeds are also scattered
out across the bog.

Do you feel the tension between two worlds,
Moving forever like the fairy folk?
You will not find my roots underground at all
It's in The Milky Way that I am lying.

Aodán McCardle

50 Dreams of Wolves

1

I don't know what that means. To dream of wolves or wolf dreams being the dreams wolves have. Wolves do dream. Anyone who has a dog knows that they dream, and they run in their dreams, in their sleep, so 50 dreams of wolves could be dreams about wolves, could be wolves dreaming or

2

The chase. Wolves running. Is it all about hunger? Are all our dreams about hunger? Have we just made everything more complicated than it needs to be? Is hunger the basic drive? Is this what farming gave us, time to consider something other than hunger? Did sex interrupt hunger or is it just another type of hunger? Is power another type of hunger? Are sex and power only developments of hunger bred out of those moments farming gave us of structured eating, structured satiation? The very idea of structured satiation leads to sex and power.

3

I dream of wolves. I dream that they are chasing me. I kick the clothes off the bed trying to get away. I once kicked my wife while running from wolves but she didn't bite me. That's why I am still here, still dreaming of wolves but still here. But what do wolves dream of, not of me, but what?

4

Here's the thing though, a wolf would tear your head off and eat you and it would be the right thing to do. It would suckle on the blood from your heart and with it your love, your liver, the temperament of your day, your spleen enlarged by its exposure on social media, your brain's pulsed thoughts still dreaming and it would be the right thing to do. Why should a wolf dream of harmony and love? Why shouldn't a wolf dream of blood!

5

My son shouts, screams, his frustration and distress and disgust into the microphone on his headphones or his Playstation or his PC. He rails against the slow erosion of his time by school, the years ahead that seem filled already with duties like homework, for him the length of a day relates to what he has to do and all the time he might have to do it. He can't weigh the length of a day in hours and minutes, it's weighed in years of future ties. His dreams are filled with what he cannot get away from, not of wolves, if he dreamed of wolves it would be better.

6

What is the difference between writing as a wolf or writing as a dog. Writing as anyone other than yourself is problematic. Interpretation can be right and wrong. It must be worth it to be wrong. But the dog has none of the rights of the wolf it seems. The wolf has a space and place of its own if only in our minds, a language and will that make intrusion a transgression. The dog has only what we give it and our only transgression is when we eat it.

7

The young wolves choose to stay to help out. The leader isn't the leader because they dominate the pack. When we look into darkness we use our own eyes.

8

I'm not sentimental about it. They did a sort of experiment. They reintroduced wolves into a national park and everything, everything, changed. The river changed direction, the variety of animals increased, they came back. Where did they come back from? The way the world worked, its balance, changed. This is a dream, that positive aspect of the word dream, but this is not a dream dream, it happened, but this is not the dream of a wolf, this is our dream but not a dream, not something to be hoped for, not a wish, this happened but while it was happening what did the wolves dream of.

9

It's a bad morning outside, a dirty day, a droch lá someone said in this case the lá comes after the droch. The sequence of language places us in the world nor separates us from the world. In dreams we are more in the world than ever. How in the world is a wolf dreaming?

10

My son showed me a story on snapchat or some other social media platform, a distinction to a degree of age, of vistas that only some will see, but anyway the gist of the story was that a you tuber, maybe an influencer, I'm not sure of the difference, but this you tuber was going to fight a boxer, not just any boxer, one who has won championships, maybe past his prime but still, anyway apparently the you tuber has fought a few others, celebrities or other you tubers or whatever. My son says he trains like mad for it. My son seems impressed by this, he doesn't say that but the fact that he's showing it to me, but I feel a loathing for it. I try not to respond negatively but I can't help it. After a moment I say that, I say that I find it despicable, that I find it pathetic that this is what people do, that this is what people take seriously. I see by his face that he's disappointed, that this judgment, my judgment seems to reflect on him but he's a young teenager and I say that, I say to him that it's no judgment on him, that it's these people with power, a modicum of celebrity, with some status, that it's them my judgment is for but still I know it's hit him too so I make sure to do what I can to assuage that and

I think well if these two were wolves they'd probably do just this, they'd square up to each other, even if not a fight to the death they'd do it just to show off at least, to test the moment and I think why then should I judge them any different... but I know that I still feel the same, the risks for the wolves are something they'll live with but these two

11

what is the difference between planning, planning for and experience which suggests future possibilities, do wolves plan for, is there evidence of future possibilities, is the answer good or bad, is it the same or worse than, is it an indication of, a suggestion that, is there a comparison to be made, I've noticed just now while mistyping that there is a prison in comparison but I don't know what is kept there, perhaps that's where the dreams of wolves are kept, all prisons are made to be escaped from

12

Are there things a wolf won't do? Why? What would I not do? There are things I think I can't write about but I can't get close enough to them to know if I would or not and I suspect if prompted that I might but right now I don't know but I am not a wolf but why would a wolf not do some things, is it fear, is fear just a survival mechanism, would I not write about some things because of the survival mechanism, do they not smell right, if I saw someone else eating would I eat too.

13

territory, what is territory, how do we think of a wolf as having territory, is ownership anything to do with territory, is territory spatial or is it things, things to eat, is eating and the collection of materials within a space the necessary paraphernalia to achieve sexual congress, is sex only procreation, is the act itself only a means to an end, the wolf doesn't seek to mate unless to procreate, is there futurity or only instinct or are both simultaneous, is being part of a group important and can it be any group or only those related or those with whom future relations might be expected so what sort of a group is it? There are people in most groups who I don't like or trust or who don't like me and maybe I like them fine but they don't like me and maybe they've never really met me and I wonder why, why don't they like me, or trust, why don't they trust me, maybe I'm too careful, I only stay in the group long enough to say hello, to greet, to swap some language, I want everyone to like me or I'd like everyone to like me which isn't the same and maybe I don't really want to get to know everyone but I see that some people who've never met get on and I've been standing there and there's a distance and I can't name that distance, if I could name it I might be able to do something about it but eventually like this sentence I've been in it too long and whatever I was going to say or do the pressure becomes too much and I run and hide

14

How bright is brightness for a wolf? Is brightness just something that makes seeing easier or is it something that makes being seen easier? I watched a story about her crossing the Alps, about her drive to survive. What I remember are slopes, sloping one way and then the other. What I remember are rocks, rocks and snow. What I remember is looking, always looking, the story could not contain the olfactory but it made looking an ongoing, eyes always open, always working and lines always sloping, somewhere here in the whiteness, hidden behind the black scree, looking out continuously looking out.

15

Today things were pulled from under me, onwardness was arrested, the moment wreaked of caution, of stillness and waiting. In itself it was explainable, reasonable, but in the midst of all the rest of this, of all these thrown punches, of this everyday of wariness, then, then, there's always the possibility of worse out of the side of the eye, always just a little breath held, always a tightness. Today didn't become any worse, not yet.

16

How to get from A to B. First of all not knowing when B is is important. Take a step, take another, wait, go back, wait, what language are we using here, why becomes more important if its reason for being is either desire or hunger. Why can be found at various stations, it moves just like any animal taking up position based on either need or fear. I might have a why that relates to your why but that doesn't mean we are friends. Your dream of freedom and my dream of freedom might not align. One might depend upon the other but one might depend upon the other. One might depend upon the other. Your dream of freedom, your dream of freedom, one free from the other... B might be a why or it might be a how. B might be a dream, B might be a desire, B might be or it might not. B might be found on the way to B. B might begin by being heard, it might be seen or seen in the mind's eye. Scented once then B might become something else entirely. A is mobile, it may have been there but it may become now. A is just this side of B but may be simply what B isn't. It may be before B or it might come after, the before of another B. How to get from A to B, take a step, run...

17

One can ferret but can one wolf? Apparently yes. Cry wolf (too often) the dictionary advises, "hold a ~ by the ears," "keep the ~ from the door," "lone ~ ," "~in sheep's clothing," "throw to the ~s," not quite but "to devour or swallow greedily," one can wolf but really is that it, to wolf, I saw them playing with a traffic cone in the snow, I mean I wasn't there, in person, in the snow, it was on twitter, yes there are wolves on twitter, these were young male wild wolves, like wolves wolves and they had an orange conical traffic cone, as urban and domestic as you like except of course at night out there on the motorways, on the roads, in

AODÁN MCCARDLE

the dark, the traffic cones stand witness, still present... but here in the snow, the young male wolves chase each other for this cone dragged out of its solitary station into this playful present. Joy! To wolf then can be to joy! To find inordinate pleasure in the mundane, in the, dysfunctional is not the word, unpurposeful is not the word, rún in Irish passes between purpose and mystery and even love, to "mean to" and yet remain the act of the secret, these wolves are [rún]ning in the snow and all that they are are(ing) is a mystery. To Joy! To Wolf! To joy!

18

when I'm writing I live along or near a dictionary, in fact a small stand of dictionaries, it's more than a copse, they're of different ages and their leaves have different markings, different roots, [wood] not be found together except in the vernacular, in the local functional of doing and being done and I think the wolf must have a dictionary, a thing to read when trying to understand a thing but then so many words in the local doingness of my childhood remained outside the classroom, quite clear in their meaning without any definition or spelling. Some I later realized were the language of the other, hiding in our everyday lives, hiding in our doings so long that those who passed them down to us no longer knew where they'd come from and yet we understood, so in the gaps between the trees are the words and their definitions are found in the doing. The wolf's dictionary is in its doing, in its doing with others, the wolf dictionary is the other.

19

So then can a wolf dream while it's awake. If it does not look for meaning for definition, if its everyday is the uncertain then what is the difference between dreaming and waking. To exist indefinably between the two, awake and asleep are different physical conditions and not different conditions of the dream. When I was young there was a dog, a long haired dog, running across a field, a steep sloping field, it was running always from right to left up across a sloping field in the near distance and always it was around the middle of the field running and always I woke up with my heart beating fast. A nightmare? But there was nothing to fear. I knew I would see it again, not when but as certainly as the sun coming up I knew that I would see it again and I knew that I would wake up with my heart beating fast. Why was the dog running? Why did the sight of the dog running make my heart beat fast? Why did it wake me, did I wake when watching when seeing, when looking at this dog running, this long haired dog running up across the sloping field in the distance. As I think about it now years later, I can clearly see the dog, I can clearly see the field and I realize that yes it was a field but it was also a clearance. The field, a big field, was surrounded by a dark tone at the edge of view and I realize that the darkness was trees or the trees were shadowed and the dog was in the middle of the field, in the middle of the clearance, in the open. The middle of the clearance, the open, is a place where the heart beats faster.

20

an old wolf knows that before getting out of the car you should move the seat back. It makes it easier to get out. It makes it easier to get in. what would an old human know that makes life easier. One of those things that just take a bit of thought, an effort that relieves effort. An action that is really nothing within the ongoing of actions but just makes everything easier. What does the old wolf do that just changes the passage? How would we know? I saw the young males, they had cornered an elk, it was there surrounded and yet... at some point in the ongoing of that day of that passage between light and dark of that moment the young wolves realized that the Elk had them surrounded, with its back to the cliff, to that gaping space the Elk had played a gambit and won. What would an old elk do?

21

The female moved

22

Summer is nearly gone more in its socially organized late early 21st century than in its seasonal early or mid and hopefully not late climate change blue dot Perseid shower era. Is it was it a time of plenty, for the wolves? Was it a time of plenty? Is it what a wolf would dream of? A time of Plenty? Would a wolf dream of a time of plenty or is that a human sense of things? Would a wolf dream of the chase or of the bloated moments after the chase, after the gorge, when the belly is full? Would a wolf ever evolve as far as TV dinners and Reality TV? Or is that also just a blind alley?

23

So... it's a family thing, it appears anyway. This big group organized alpha lead strike team is peculiar it seems to specific locale, to specific prey perhaps. For the rest it's about family, Mother and Father and young. Dreams then might not simply be the chase, the hunt, the kill. Dreams might just be about family. I wonder are there any anarchist or anti-capitalist wolves or is it just that there is no need for them. Someone somewhere said it was the horse, that it was the horse changed our dreams to conquest. Someone else said it was farming, that it was wheat, or a peculiarity of gene adaptation in grasses at the end of the last ice age that allowed us to sow but every people had gardens of a kind, forest gardens, desert gardens and people lived close to animals long before the horse was used for conquest so what changed our dreams to this... now.

24

I waited a long time for another dream and then I waited just as long to write it down. In between was a wandering, a migration, of the mind, a leaving of this world to dwell... elsewhere. But lately I've wanted to come back and as usual it took a break, a break in routine to get here but the dream happened before the migration and it wasn't wolves, it was lions, or lion cubs, two of them, small and inquisitive and I remember sitting, lying, there, on the rock, and they scrambled up over the edge and stumbled towards me, us, me, it was me, but felt like an us, and briefly it was amazing and then I thought, lion cubs, out on their own, so dangerous, and I thought, they're not going to be on their own, there are going to be lions where there are lion cubs, and there they were, the lions, just coming into view under the trees, whether the trees were there before I noticed the lions under them I'm not sure but there they were and under them the lions, coming towards me, us, me and I thought where's the car, there must be a car and there just to one side, just outside the eyeline, there was the car and I thought I won't make it on time, but it was just there and they were coming closer but it was even closer but I knew, I knew I wouldn't make it, like wading through thick air, and I knew, this is a dream but still I knew that it would just get harder and harder to reach the car and that this was a dream, like my own head torturing me, getting some strange pleasure from making me fear, and then I woke up and I knew that it was a dream and that it wasn't real and still I couldn't sleep.

25

The tracker showed images of a young wolf playing in the snow, pushing its front legs deep into the drift and then submerging its nose, a part of me knows this play will be useful when it hunts for mice and rodents or is that foxes but then if foxes why not wolves but another part of me can only think that that will be cold and wet, how kids can enjoy this stuff without thinking about the clothes that will need to be sorted, soggy and dripping, how I went out in wellingtons as a kid into heavy snow all morning without socks and when I came in my feet were red and numb and later my big toe nails went black and fell off. I want to tell the wolf to be careful and I want to be the wolf

26

And now time has passed and the Bears are disappearing off into slumber again rolled in a year's bounty so soon so soon while the wolves alert keep watch keep watch awake awake to this dream.

　　　　　　　　　　　　　　　　　　　　　　AODÁN MCCARDLE

Author's note:

My writing practice in general is one that places improvisation to the fore as a dynamic. This displaces, for me anyway, the author as the centre of control and instead casts them into an atmosphere of forces, ideas, things which constantly change as life winds its merry way into the future. Within each type of writing, poetry, critical, short fiction/essay, modes of address tend to retain stronger resonance so for instance sentence structure might have a greater influence in one than in the other. Content, authorial aspiration to write about something, tends to be buffeted fairly strongly while latent concerns from the everyday experience of the world tend to emerge stubbornly often whatever the context. I might set out to write something closer to a short story, I might have in mind a 1000 words or 2000 words and one paragraph in the piece is done. Much of my short fiction/essay work begins as an object or a title from which I improvise, in the case of 50 Dreams about Wolves the title came in part from a conversation with my daughter, possibly about art or writing or possibly dreams, she would have been 11 or 12 at the time, and the number itself seemed to resonate, I knew from the start that the number wouldn't change just as when an object comes into view in a certain way, resonates is the best description I have for it, then I know I'll eventually write about that or use it as the beginning of an improvisation. The writing grows one line or usually one paragraph at a time and apart from spelling mistakes or in the case of a particularly impatient paragraph where it demands to be put down quicker than I can type and I get the word rhythm wrong, I don't go back to edit, I don't change something just because I don't like where it's going, I don't exclude something because I'm uncomfortable with it, i hang on and try to negotiate with it as it's happening, to understand it and what its saying, what it's saying in the sense of what it wants or means. Two writers who are very different and to a degree don't seem to relate to my writing at all influenced me in this even before improvisation became a central dynamic in my work. JRR Tolkien, I read somewhere, and in both cases I'm paraphrasing, said that he met Strider in the Autumn and it was much later that he realized who he was, and Harold Pinter said that he realized that a character would remain, would stay, when it began speaking back, began to resist his attempts to manipulate or make it do things. So 50 Dreams about Wolves, while it retains that number as a sense of map or scale may or may not become 50 paragraphs but it planted the idea of numbering the paragraphs and that in turn emphasises an order to those paragraphs where in another piece of writing the reader might think the order of the paragraphs is malleable. It occurs to me that some of those 50 dreams may be ones I never have, some of the paragraphs are based on actual dreams and some are events, information, experiences that are drawn to or emerge in this piece of writing but the idea that they are all dreams and this changes how we understand what is real or not real or why there is a distinction is another strong resonance from that title, an example of how something comes to form meanings and potentials of its own when the author is no longer the only one with a voice. Dream 26 did happen as the bears went into hibernation and I've wondered how the wolves are doing and survive and I have been waiting for them to come back and then one day somewhere in the social media stratosphere or traditional media I came across some adult wolves playing in the snow, they revelled in it in a way that children do while in my mind the winter must be a time of hunger and I thought that we adults, humans, have so much wrong in how we face each day. I don't sentimentalize nature or apply spirituality to nature but this piece of writing does question my relation to it, it being life in general.

Extracts 1, 3, 8 and 19 were published in *Becoming-Feral*, University of Wisconsin-Maddison and Royal Conservatoire of Scotland: Objet-a Creative Studio 2021.

AODÁN MCCARDLE

Jaye Nasir

Among the Mangroves

Counting the seconds between
flashes of lightning as
something big skims the water's surface
from below. They go back, we go on
into the forest's mouth. Wet hair against
wet skin, cold rain stippling the warm sea
like goose flesh. Avery is afraid
until she isn't. The downpour grows
so loud that we can hardly hear
the others speak, but we do
hear the mangroves, their silence
which is just another word
for time. Vultures watch us
from the treetops, rarely a good omen,
but sometimes—times like this:
my clothes soaked, fists clenched
on the oars, water rising over the roots
too fast—I see everything that frightens me
as proof of life. We could die here,
she says, but with the thunder swallowing
our laughter, fog falling over the hills
like sleep settling over a body in a bed
of early dusk, what it means
to me is: we are unkillable.

Jaye Nasir

The Meadow

It recurs, the dream that is having
me. An allegory that falls
apart halfway through, fable without
any moral. Metaphor so mixed
it's turning colors, pale greens and pinks
and grays. It goes something like:

The bees are kissing the clover
and the clover is kissing back.

Like: the meadow is eternal. Fallow
in pale sunshine. Winter is only a quality of light
like everything else. Summer, a long blurry
something, with nights so shallow
you can wade through them, barefoot,
naked from the brain down. Blood blooming
from in between your—

Go ahead and say thighs. Nobody is listening.

I guess you can say lips or nail beds
or wherever your blood happens
to be pouring out of. Whatever the wound,
whatever the tongue to lick it.
Go ahead and say clover flowers.

Say foxglove, say dandelion full of unspent
wishes. Swaying on thin stems, faces
all turned toward the sun. It used to be
that I could only write about winter.

It used to be that way.

Now the wind is in my hair, smelling
of light, wetting my sodden
appetite. Shudder of a body wracked
with sobs: that's winter. I have this relationship
with winter, and this long memory
that belongs to the ground.

Don't worry, we'll wreathe you
in flowers. Build you a casket
of flowers and the bees, the butterflies,
the hummingbirds will drink.

The most that you can do for this world is to die.

That's the gift. Don't call it an ending.
Close your eyes, feel your eyelashes
brushing your cheeks. You don't
have to call it anything at all.
The ground will not ask you. The bees
and the butterflies will not ask.

Jennifer LoveGrove

Pantone Colour of the Year

I don't need the sea
to rub her salt over my limbs
crusting up my hair to hear
her roar or is that me
proclaiming the five stages
of drowning again, no
it's the coral chanting underwater
telling us how it sounds
to want to stay alive:
not today not today not today
not today at least not today.

I like raspberries do you
like raspberries? I want to visit
Chefchauen do you
want to visit Chefchauen?
On Saturday I raked the garden beds
and tore out the tiny
blue flowers I swear
I didn't mean to.

Pantone Classic Blue, *a colour that*
anticipates what's going to happen next.
When asked why we were not warned
the 2020 colour of the year
declined to comment just
kept pulsing wet pores
slurping in more of the day
after the day after the day after
the day after the day after that.

At least there are still Malbecs
and monologues, bonfires and wild ginger,
wait, that's toxic, run through
with arsenic and pipelines
voter suppression and cut
cables, liars who just happen to be
a little bit taller than you
I mean me, anyway
I meant wild leeks
and watercress as a child

I liked the television shows
that old people watched,
quiet golf tournaments
where everyone spoke in hushed tones
under their breath as though
afraid to name what was happening
lest it keep rolling down that hill
faster and faster and faster and faster
than the cameras could track
glowing hot and racing
across the country to the coast
then cliff diving straight to the bottom
of the sea, hissing softly.

Notes on Contributors

Is file í Julie Breathnach-Banwait. Tá dhá leabhar filíochta curtha i gcló ag Coisceim léi, *Dantá Póca* i 2020 agus *Ar thóir gach ní* i 2022. Tógadh na prós dhanta seo as leabhar nua prósfhiliochta dátheangach léi *Cnámha Scoilte* a bheas á fhoilsiú i 2023. Tá conaí uirthi sa Tasmáin lena clann.

Susan Bruce has a Masters of Fine Arts in Acting from New York University. She performed on Broadway, off Broadway and regionally for over twenty years. Susan has studied poetry at The New School with Patricia Carlin, Kathleen Ossip and David Lehman. She has two chapbooks, both published by Finishing Line Press, the second due out in a year. Her poems have been online and in print in many publications including the following: *Love's Executive Order*, *SWWIM*, *Arcturus* (University of Chicago) Driftwood Press, *Luna Luna*, Yes Books, *Barrow Street*, *Washington Square Review*, *805 Lit & Art*, *No Dear*, *Finery*, *Dirty Chai*, *Scarlet Leaf Review* and Regal House Publishing. Susan spends as much time near the water as she can. She is a surfer and an avid swimmer. She is 99% made of water.

Dr. Alicia Byrne Keane is a Pushcart Prize-nominated poet, with writing published in *The Moth*, *Banshee*, *The Stinging Fly* and *Anthropocene*, among other journals. Further writing is forthcoming in *The Seneca Review* and *The Colorado Review*; Alicia's debut collection will be published by Broken Sleep Books in December 2023.

Gemma Cooper-Novack is a queer writer whose debut poetry collection *We Might As Well Be Underwater* (Unsolicited Press, 2017) was a finalist for the CNY Book Award. She's published chapbooks with Warren Tales and The Head & the Hand. Her poetry and fiction have appeared in more than forty journals; her plays have been produced across the United States. She is a Deming Fund grantee and a Visiting Assistant Professor in Literacy Education at Hobart & William Smith Colleges.

Ion Corcos was born in Sydney, Australia in 1969. He has been published in *Cordite, Meanjin, Wild Court, riddlebird, The Sunlight Press*, and other journals. Ion is a nature lover and a supporter of animal rights. He is the author of *A Spoon of Honey* (Flutter Press, 2018).

Seth Crook lives on Mull, loves sea slugs, has taught philosophy at various universities. His poems have appeared in such places as *The Rialto, Magma, Pennine Platform, Northwords Now, Poetry Scotland, Poetry Salzburg Review, Channel*. In e-zines such as *Tentacular, Streetcake*. In recent anthologies such as *The SHOp: An Anthology* (Liffey), *A470* (Arachne), *The Centenary Collection* (Speculative), *Places of Poetry* (One World). He has a pamphlet of visual poems *Chalked On The Path* (Dreich).

Agnieszka Filipek is a Polish-born poet living in Ireland. Her work has been published worldwide. Her poems have appeared in *Amsterdam Quarterly, SAND Journal, Capsule Stories, Local Wonders Anthology, Lucent Dreaming, Black Bough Poetry, Crannóg, Chrysanthemum, Autumn Sky Poetry Daily, The Stony Thursday Book, Balloons Literary Journal*, and elsewhere.

Alicia Hilton is an author, editor, arbitrator, law professor, actor, and former FBI Special Agent. She believes in angels and demons, magic, and monsters. Her work has appeared or is forthcoming in Akashic Books, *Daily Science Fiction, Lovecraftiana, Neon, NonBinary Review, Space and Time, Unnerving, Vastarien, Year's Best Hardcore Horror Volumes 4, 5 & 6*, and elsewhere. Alicia's website is https://aliciahilton.com.

Jason Kennealy is a writer from Tramore, Co. Waterford.

Susan Lanigan is a historical novelist and the author of *White Feathers* (2014) and *Lucia's War* (2020). In addition, she has been thrice shortlisted for the Hennessy New Irish Writing awards and has had short fiction published in a variety of outlets. A Green Party member since 2017 and former LEA, she maintains a passionate interest in environmental issues. She lives by the sea in East Cork.

Barbara Lock, a writer, editor, teacher, and emergency physician, teaches at Columbia University Vagelos College of Physicians and Surgeons in New York City. There's more about her at barbaralock.com.

Jennifer LoveGrove is the author of, most recently, the poetry chapbook *The Tinder Sonnets* and the collection *Beautiful Children with Pet Foxes*. Her novel *Watch How We Walk* was longlisted for the Scotiabank Giller Prize. She is currently working on a full-length poetry manuscript and a new novel. She works at the University of Toronto.

Aodán McCardle's current practice is improvised performance/writing/drawing. His PhD is on 'Action as Articulation of the Contemporary Poem.' He has two books, *Shuddered* and *ISing*, from VEER Books, an online chapbook, *LllOoVvee*, from Smithereens Press, and a new 2023 book, *Small Increments*, from BeirBua Press. @redochretattoo on instagram, @redochre1 on twitter.

Beth McDonough's poetry is widely anthologised and published. She reviews for DURA and elsewhere. Her first solo pamphlet *Lamping for pickled fish* is published by 4Word. She has a site-specific poem on the Corbenic Poetry Path. Makar of the FWS in 2022, she's busy on a hybrid project on outdoor swimming.

Is amhránaí, file agus scríobhneoir ilteangach í Amano Miura. Rugadh in iardheisceart na Seapáine agus tógadh in iardheisceart na hÉireann í. Bíonn sí ag plé le téamaí aitheantais, grá, cultúir, draíochta agus dúchais. Tá a leithéid de thaisteal déanta aici ar fud an domhain, ach fós is é timpeallacht conntae Chiarraí, a ceantar dúchasach, an foinse ionsparáide is láidre atá ag Amano. Tá máistreacht san oidhreacht agus caomhú idir láimhe aici i gColáiste Ollscoile Baile Átha Cliath faoi láthair agus tá sí ag tnúth go mór le díriú ar chúrsaí ceoil agus scríobhneoireachta tar éis di an chéim a bhaint amach.

Jaye Nasir is a poet and writer from Portland, OR, whose work blurs, or outright ignores, the line between the real and the unreal. Her writing has appeared in many small publications, both local and international, including *Moss: A Journal of the Pacific Northwest*, *Santa Clara Review*, and *Antithesis Journal*.

Nils Nelson earned a Masters degree in Creative Writing at California State, Fresno, 1974. An avid golfer, his award-winning writing has appeared in numerous golf magazines in the U.S. Nils lives in Tucson, Arizona, where he's polishing a full-length poetry manuscript and burning through sunscreen.

Is file agus scríbhneoir é Keev Ó Baoill (siad/é) atá bunaithe i mBaile Átha Cliath. Is file aiteach, tras agus néara-éagsúil é agus tá a chuid oibre bunaithe ar na heispéiris sin agus an chaoi go mbíonn éifeachtaí ag na heispéiris sin ar a shaol laethúil. Tá a chuid scríbhneoireacht foilsithe in *Powders Press*, *The Places Zine*, GCN.ie, *SapphiXXX* agus in áiteachaí eile.

Gaillmheach is ea William James Ó hÍomhair agus bhí suim aige riamh sna healaíona, idir fhilíocht, dhrámaíocht agus cheol. Fuair sé a chuid léinn in Ollscoil Luimnigh agus i gColáiste na Trionóide, áiteanna ina ndearna sé staidéar ar cheol agus ar theangacha. Chuir sé spéis faoi leith in obair chruthaitheach idirchultúrtha agus an caidreamh idir an dúlra agus an duine daonna. Le blianta beaga anuas, bhain sé slí bheatha amach mar theagascóir Gaeilge sa Fhrainc, ag teagasc sa Centre Culturel Irlandais i bPáras, chomh maith le Université de Bretagne Occidentale, sa Bhriotáin in ábhair a bhaineann leis an teanga, a stair agus a litríocht. Taobh leis sin, tá sé an-tiomanta do ghníomhachas comhshaoil agus gníomhachas sóisialta araon. Tugann sé faoi cheisteanna na féiniúlachta a iniúchadh san Eoraip chomhaimseartha chomh maith le freagraíochtaí comhshaoil an duine dhaonna.

Is as baile beag in aice le Philadelphia, Pennsylvania do Mhaidhc Ó Maolmhuaidh (Mike Malloy), áit ar fhoghlaim sé a chuid Gaeilge (agus Laidine) ar dtús báire. Chaith sé seal ina chónaí thar lear ag múineadh Béarla, agus oibríonn sé anois mar chomhordaitheoir in ollscoil. Tá cónaí air i bPhiladelphia lena bhean chéile, Lauren, agus a iníon, Eleanor. Bíonn sé gníomhach sa ghrúpa 'Gaeilgeoirí Philadelphia' ar Facebook.

David Ishaya Osu is a poet, memoirist and street photographer living in South Australia. He is currently undertaking a PhD in Creative Writing at the University of Adelaide

Rory O'Sullivan is from Cork and lives in Dublin, where he does a PhD in ancient Greek literature. His poetry has appeared in *Channel* several times as well as Dedalus Press, *Skylight 47*, and other places. He writes occasional reviews for *Village Magazine*.

Stella Reed (she/her) is the co-author of *We Are Meant to Carry Water*, from 3: A Taos Press, and the winner of Jacar Press' Chapbook Prize for *Myth from the field where the fox runs with its tail on fire*. Stella is a novice beekeeper from Santa Fe, NM.

Martha Ryan is an emerging writer. She is currently an MFA student at the University of Washington, Seattle, USA. Her work has been published or is forthcoming in *Foglifter*, *Fugue*, and a smattering of academic journals.

Joel Scarfe is widely published. His poems feature internationally in magazines, anthologies and periodicals. He lives in Bristol UK with the Danish ceramicist Rebecca Edelmann and their two children.

G.G. Silverman is a female-identifying author who lives just north of Seattle. She is also disabled and the daughter of Italian immigrants. She loves writing lyrical short fiction that pierces the heart. For more info, please visit www.ggsilverman.com.

Anna Teresa Slater is a teacher from Iloilo, Philippines. She completed her MA in Creative Writing at Lancaster University. Anna's work is published in various international journals and anthologies. Her first poetry collection, *A Singular, Spectacular Chore*, was published in 2022.

Hailing from Raton, New Mexico (USA), Padma Thornlyre has composed poetry for fifty-one years and published nine collections, most recently the four books of *The Anxiety Quartet*. The poems included here are included in the appendix to his first novel, *Baubo's Beach*, for which Padma is actively seeking an agent.

Athira Unni is a PhD candidate and poet living in Leeds, UK. Her first book of poetry *Gaea and Other Poems* was published in 2020. She is the founder and Poetry Editor of *Qissa* magazine. She appreciates a good evening sky and is fascinated by octopuses.

Monica Wang has writing in *Electric Lit*, *Southword*, *Malahat Review*, and *Banshee*. In 2022 she was shortlisted for the W&A Working-Class Writers' Prize while completing her MA. Born in Taichung, Taiwan, she grew up in Taipei and Vancouver, Canada, and spent the last five years drifting from Dresden to Dublin.

Thank you to our generous patrons

Hannah Gaden Gilmartin
Ed Madden
Sara Nishikawa

We also want to thank those patrons who wish to remain anonymous.